The Ranch

KELLY POSTERT

This book is dedicated to my Mom, Ellen, who has been my biggest supporter. She was unable to see me actually publish this book. I know she is sitting up there reading her own copy and telling everyone who would listen how proud she is of me. I love you Mama and may you be visiting your own Ranch up there.

To my unconventional bestie/sister Chassidy: What a road we have walked both figuratively and literally. I know how much you loved this book. Finally you get to share these characters with others.

To Mack and my girls. I love you all and thank you for being there to support me each step of the way.

Author book
The Ranch

Cover design by Cover a Book
Edited by Twin Tweaks Editing
Self-published

CONTENTS

CHAPTER 1

He couldn't believe it had been almost four weeks since his wife Allison just up and left him. She took off with no word and no warning. He had gone to town to get a load of wood to fix the roof of the barn and when he got back, all her stuff was gone. All that was left as a damn note saying she will always love him. He called the Diner to see if her Aunt Linda or anyone else had seen her; if they had, no one was talking. Her aunt did mention she felt she was unhappy, but wouldn't say more than that. Sitting at his desk, he was going over the past couple of months in his mind trying to see if he missed any clues that she was unhappy. The ringing of the phone brought him out of his thoughts.

"LJ Ranch."

"Yes, may I speak to Lionel or Allison James please?"

"This is Lionel." He responded.

"This is Maria De La Garza from Child Protective Services. I have an application for when you and your wife signed up to be foster parents. Would you be able to take in a child? I have a child in need of a home as early as Friday." It took Lionel a few seconds to answer. He had forgotten about Allison signing them up to be foster parents.

"Ms. De La Garza, my wife left me about a month ago. This whole fostering thing was her idea. I'm just a single man with nothing but a ranch."

"Mr. James, I have a very serious situation here. We have a ten-year-old boy who was taken from his family. His father violently beat him and sadly, this is not the first time. He's due to be released from the hospital in about two days and we have nowhere else for this child to go. I had a family lined up but something came up and they are not able to care for the child. He's a good boy. At this time, he does have some anger issues, which is expected with the life he has been living. We will provide counseling for him. Mr. James, are you sure there's no way that you can help us out?"

Damn, Lionel thought to himself, who could hurt a little boy like that, much less their own child? Maria said he would be released from the hospital; if he's in the hospital what in the hell did the dad do to this kid?

"Ms. De La Garza like I said my wife left me. But I have twenty ranch hands. They are good people who I know will help me watch over the kid. We'll be ready for him on Friday."

"Mr. James! Thank you so much." Maria said with a relieved breath. "I'm sorry to hear about your wife leaving, but I'm sure you will be more than helpful to this young man. The child, Scott Wilson, should be released sometime on Friday. You will get a call tomorrow with more information on his injuries and aftercare as well as his case. Again, I truly appreciate your help with Scott. If you have any questions, you can give me a call back at this number anytime, day or night."

"I'm sure we will have everything ready for Scott and I look forward to hearing from you."

Lionel hung up the phone and sat in his office trying to think about what needed to be done to get ready for the boy. First he needed to fix up a room for Scott to sleep in. Then he needed to let the ranch hands know about the situation; he would have to tell them they would be helping to watch over a child. He was unsure about how his men would handle having a young boy running around the ranch. He'd barely survived these last four weeks alone and now he would be in charge of taking care of a kid. God help this child with him in charge. If it wasn't for his neighbors, Joe and

Rose, at the J&R ranch he didn't know what he would have done. Rose had been a tremendous help by bringing left-overs and doing some light house cleaning.

Lionel decided he might as well get started. He walked around the ranch to gather up all his men. He called them up to the back porch so he could make sure they were all able to hear him. When he had all twenty men gathered around, he explained the situation to everyone.

"We will have a young man here for the unforeseeable future. You will treat him with respect. No matter if he gets underfoot, you will not show any anger towards him. He's ten years old, and he's coming from a very bad situation. As we speak, he's in the hospital from a beating at the hands of his own father."

The ranch hands start calling out threats toward the dad.

"I wanna meet this father, my fist to his face."

"Let's see how he does around here. We all have a few things we can teach that guy about being a man." Finally Lionel raised his hand to stop the guys.

"I understand your anger. Trust me. I feel the same way." Lionel continued talking to his crew. "If I find out any of you scared, yelled at, hit or threatened that boy, I will fire you on the spot. Do y'all understand me?" Lionel made eye contact with each and every ranch hand to make sure they acknowledged him. Each man gave him a nod. "Does anyone have any issues or questions? If you're not a kid friendly person let me know now. You won't lose your job over this, but I will protect this child." Charles, one of the newest ranch hands raised his hand.

"Lionel, Sir. I like kids enough, it just seems that kids don't like me." Some of the men laughed and made jokes.

"Maybe it is your face they don't like." After a few more minutes of picking on each other Lionel again got his men's attention.

"Each of y'all will have the added job of protecting this child." Lionel waited for anyone else to speak. "Great, if you have any questions or ideas, you know my home and office are always open. Truth is, I have no idea what to do with a young boy. I know that when I was a young boy I sure gave Tank a hard time." Tank loudly grumbled his agreement. "Luckily he's a great guy and let bygones be bygones. Go on back to work now, time is money and you're all standing around wasting my money." Everyone laughed. Sure Lionel had money, but he was so generous with it. He was a really great boss that took extra good care of his employees. When all the men started to walk off back to their jobs Lionel called out. "Tank, can I talk to you in my office for a minute?". They both walked into the home office. They had an office out in the barn, but Lionel liked the ranch hands to feel like it belonged to them.

"I'm going crazy." Lionel explained as he walked around his office. "What am I doing bringing in a young child now? I'm in no shape to help anyone. Hell most of the time you have to come drag my ass out of bed." Lionel looked at Tank with a mixture or concern and desperation in his eyes.

"Lionel, that boy needs you. I don't know this kid, but maybe being here is what he needs. I mean it has to be better than going back to his dad. Just man up Lionel, and do the right thing.

"Am I doing the right thing? I told her no at first because of Ally leaving me. That's when she told me about his father beating him. Tank, what kind of sick son of a bitch would hurt his own son?" Tank just shook his head. It was hard to wrap his head around something like that. Tank was a man of few words. If he spoke to you, you had better listen. So when Tank began to speak, Lionel knew to listen.

"Look Lionel, We've known each other for most of our lives. We haven't always seen eye to eye and some of the time we still don't. You have changed and in my opinion it's all been for the better. I know how hard it was for you to lose Ally. She made you happy. I never really thought she fit in around here." Lionel started to go argue about Ally, but Tank stopped him by putting up a hand and continued. "Don't get me wrong she tried, but you know she was a city girl forced to live in the country. That being said, I won't bring her up again. She's gone, and the ranch needs you back." Lionel silently just shook his head in acknowledgement. "There's a kid who needs you, and I bet you need him as well. So what you're going to do is get things ready for him."

Lionel just looked at Tank. He wasn't sure what to say. He never thought about it, but it was true. Ally grew up in the city and only moved here after her dad had passed away. She didn't choose life in the country, it was forced on her. He also knew the same thing was going to happen to Scott. What they needed to do was bring some city to the country, but was unsure how to do that. Shaking his head once, Lionel sat behind his desk and started brainstorming.

"Your right Tank. Thanks, man. You always tell me straight what I need to hear. Since he's a city boy, I'm assuming he has no experience with horses. I'll need you to teach him to ride a horse."

"I was already thinking about that boss. I'm thinking of putting him on Dreamer. You need to know how to ride to do almost anything on this ranch." Tank answered.

"I'm trusting you to take charge of this boy. At least while working outside. Can you do that?"

"Yes sir, boss." Tank confirmed with a small smile and a shake of his head.

"Great, now as for his abilities, I'm not sure what all he'll be able to do at this point. He'll be released from the hospital and straight to my custody. He should be here as early as Friday. I was warned that the boy has some anger issues. Keep an extra eye on the ranch hands to be sure they don't provoke him in any way." Tank nodded his head in agreement.

"I think a kid would be good for some of these men. I'll definitely keep an eye out. If I see he's underfoot, I promise, I'll find him something else to do." Tank answered.

"Great! Now I guess I better call Rose up and see if she is willing to help us. Lord knows we're going to need her now more than ever." Lionel told Tank. A few minutes later Tank left to go back to his ranch duties. Lionel sat at his desk and took a deep breath. Rose Murdock was his next door neighbor and had been a godsend since Ally left. Lionel picked up the phone and called her.

"Rose, this is Lionel. That was a very tasty roast you cooked up last night. Thanks again for all you've done for me. I really appreciate everything."

"Oh, Lionel it was no problem. That's what neighbors are for. Besides with Joe out of town I wouldn't know what to do with myself."

"Joe should be home next week. Then what will I eat?" After they both kind of laughed. Lionel got to the point of the call. "The reason I was calling was to ask for some help. I know I have no business asking for even more help but-."

"Lionel please! I will always try to help you whenever I can." Rose exclaimed, cutting him off.

"This is kind of important and not about me. Last year, Ally and I signed up to be foster parents."

"Oh yeah, I remember Ally was so excited and waited for that phone call to come in. She knew that it was going to be any day, but that call never came. I was so sad to see her so broken-hearted."

"Well, they called me today. Seems there's a ten-year-old who's in need of some help. At first I refused. I explained that Ally left me, but they said that it was fine. So I'm looking for a maid that can also cook, who can help look after the child. Do you possibly know of anyone who's looking for work? At this point, I'm not real picky on how well she can cook or clean." He said almost jokingly. Rose was smiling away on the other end of the line.

"Bless your soul, Lionel. I was just praying for a miracle, and here you are calling me. This call is such a blessing. I just got off the phone with my sister's daughter, Denise. She has found herself in a little situation where she's about to be homeless, and she's now jobless as well."

"Oh no, I'm so sorry to hear that. Is there anything I can do to help?" Lionel genuinely wanted to help her niece.

"She just called about an hour ago to see if we could put her up for a few months until she can get back on her feet. I told her of course we could. We just need a little time to get some money together. Plane tickets aren't cheap. My niece, bless her heart, was living with a guy out in Miami, he left her high and dry. He took all her stuff and cleaned out her bank accounts. All she has is a few sets of clothes. He even took her expensive name brand purses. I can tell you what I think of him and what I would like to do, but I'll just pray for his little Pea Picken' heart." Both Lionel and Rose were quiet for a few moments, until Lionel asked, "Can she cook and clean?"

"Of course, I taught her many of my famous dishes." Lionel thought about it for a minute.

"I can give her a job and a place to stay. If you can come over to help me out; I'll pay her way home and give her a five hundred dollar sign on bonus. But I need her to start immediately, and I need you to set it all up. Can you do that for me?"

"Oh Lionel, you are so sweet to do this for us. I'll be over in five minutes. Let me just call Denise and let her know our prayers have been answered."

They said their goodbyes and Lionel felt good. He was able to help someone else in need. He loved to be able to help people.

Reaching for a pen and paper, Lionel sat at his desk and made a list of what all he still needed to do. Once Rose arrived he showed her the list that he had made so far. She added a few things and then they decided to call so Lionel and Denise could answer each other's questions before they did anything else.

"First off, how do you feel about kids?" That was Lionel's main question.

"Um… I'm good with them unless they're newborns. I'm not so comfortable with newborns." Denise answered. Lionel explained that he needed her to cook, clean, and look after a ten-year-old boy. Then he continued on with the fact that he ran a ranch in Texas with a twenty man crew and if she was willing to start right away he would buy her a ticket to fly here and also give her a sign on bonus.

"That sounds awesome Mr. James. Yes, I'll be so happy to work for you. I'll try my best, but I do ask that you let me know if I'm messing up."

"Denise, I think we will get along just fine. As we've been speaking, your Aunt Rose has been busy setting up a flight for you. She'll be on in just a few minutes to give you all the details. I have one last question for you. I told you I would give you a signing bonus; do you want me to send it to your account or just wait and give you cash?"

"Um…" Denise was sure her aunt already told him about her boyfriend leaving her high and dry. "If you could just wait and give me cash, I'll open a new account when I get to Texas."

"Sounds good then, I'll have it ready for you when you get here. Before I give your aunt the phone, do you have any other questions for me?" Lionel asked.

"I do have one, you said that you had a twenty member crew, will I be cooking and cleaning for all of them as well?" Lionel laughed and explained that she would be cooking and cleaning for him and Scott only. Lionel handed the phone over to Rose who confirmed her flight left in five hours and she would land in Texas at six that night. After they hung up the phone, Lionel showed Rose what he was thinking about the sleeping arrangements.

"Lionel James you are just plumb crazy. How are you going to put that boy in a room with no bed? Do you have anything for him?" Lionel gave Rose that smile that let her know he was just playing with her. He knew she wouldn't allow that boy to come live in this house with no furniture.

"I have a credit card and a truck." Lionel gave her a smile that he knew she couldn't turn down.

"You're so lucky that Joe is out of town right now, or I would have to turn you down. I can't allow that young boy to come into this house with nothing."

"I agree with you Rose, that's why I called you." Lionel said with a smile.

"You better hope that your card is ready for a shopping spree, because I plan on shopping. Let's go! As a reward for helping you shop and helping you find a cook and maid, I think you're buying me lunch at Pop's Diner." Rose said jokingly.

Lionel and Rose walked through the furniture store for what felt like hours to Lionel. He never liked shopping for his furniture; he was used to just giving Allison the credit card and letting her go. He walked over to the reclining chair section and sat in one that looked comfortable. He just sat there and waited for Rose to pick everything out; they ended up with two queen size beds with matching dressers and nightstands. Then they went to Wal-Mart to buy bedding and other things that Scott and Denise might need. They held off on getting Scott clothes until they could get his sizes. Afterwards they went to Pop's Diner and had lunch. When they got back to the LJ Ranch, Lionel got two of his ranch hands to help carry all the stuff up to Scott's new room. After doing a quick clean up of the room, Rose told them where she wanted everything placed and situated. Then they walked downstairs to the maid's room, off the kitchen and again Rose did a quick cleaning and told the men where to place the items. Rose left to go tend to her own ranch and let Lionel know that she would be picking up her niece around six from the airport.

CHAPTER 2

Hours later Lionel was in his office going over emails. Maria had just sent him one about Scott and what was needed for his care. It seemed the boy was pretty healthy, minus the bruising and broken bones he suffered at the hands of his father.

"Lionel, we're here." Rose called out. Lionel walked into the living room and introduced himself to Denise.

"Welcome, I'm Lionel James, but you can call me Lionel. I can see the family resemblance. You two could pass as sisters." Lionel stated as he shook Denise's hand. Rose and Denise just laughed because they heard that all the time; Rose was only a few years older than Denise. "Let me show you around." Lionel showed her to her room as he carried her bags. Then he showed her the rest of the house. Rose, Denise, and Lionel sat at the kitchen table and talked about everything. They talked about Denise and her problems. Rose told Denise how Allison just up and left Lionel for no reason about a month ago. Denise told Lionel she understood what he was going through. Rose informed Denise that with Joe out of town a couple more days, that she would be able to help her get settled. So the two women dove into Denise's new duties, starting with making a grocery list and learning the layout of the ranch.

The next day Denise got to work early. First order of business was breakfast. She made eggs, bacon, and biscuits. Then she put on a load of laundry and started to clean up downstairs. Around noon, Lionel came into the house and asked her to come outside to the back porch. She followed him out of the kitchen door and was met with a bunch of men standing just off the porch.

"Afternoon gentlemen. I know that you have a lot of work to do and I keep stopping you, so I'll make this quick. This is Denise. I hired her to help me in the house. She's off limits." Denise blushed from embarrassment. She was not ready to start a relationship with anyone and Lionel made sure his men knew to leave her alone. "If I find out one of you so much as flirt with her I'll fire you on the spot. Do you get me?" A chorus of "Yes boss" was heard from the group. "As you go back to your jobs, please walk by Denise and introduce yourself."

The first ranchhand to introduce himself was Jim.

"Ma'am, I'm Jim. I'm mostly in charge of the cattle side of the ranch. If you need anything, my office is in the barn; the second door." Jim left and then one by one the other men walked by, shook Denise's hand, and went back to work. Tank was the last man to introduce himself.

"Name's Tank. I'm in charge of the ranch as a whole. I'm second in command, right behind Lionel. It's my job to make sure all of our employees know how to ride and care for horses. We do the majority of our work on horseback." The whole time Tank was introducing himself to Denise he just held her hand. He didn't know why he couldn't let it go. "Do you know how to ride yet?" Tank asked her.

"I have been on a horse before." Denise blushed a little as she replied. "But Joe, my uncle, was usually on with me."

"Then it'll be my pleasure to teach you to ride; if you choose to learn. My office is always open, and it's the first door in the barn." Tank looked to see that Lionel had been watching them the whole time. "I need to get back to work, but my offer still stands." Tank told Denise. As he was walking away Tank yelled over his shoulder. "Not a word Lionel, not a word." Lionel just stood quietly with a smile on his face.

Denise realized that Lionel was a good boss; he was strict but fair. She thought he was funny and could tell that he had good men working for him. The day went by uneventfully and after dinner Denise and Lionel sat on the back porch, drinking a glass of sweet tea.

"Lionel I don't think I had a chance to thank you yet. You don't know how desperate I was. I held off on calling Rose until I was completely out of options."

"Why would you wait? I've known Joe and Rose for a while now and I know they would have helped."

"Yeah they would have, but to be honest, I was embarrassed. I didn't know what to do."

"Well I am so glad you're here now. I'm so lucky that the stars aligned for us." They continued to chat. "So have you thought about what you want from life now on. Like, is this ranch a stepping stone?" Denise just looked around the ranch and just told him the truth.

"I'm so overwhelmed with life right now. I haven't thought about tomorrow, much less what I am going to do. I really do appreciate this offer and I plan to do the best I can. I'm still scared I'm going to wake up and this opportunity has been a dream." Lionel just agreed.

"I am still in awe of this whole situation myself. I think everything lined up perfectly and sometimes that can be scary. Like too good to be true."

"Exactly! That's how I'm feeling right now, like I'm waiting for the bad news or something."

"Hopefully the only bad news is the fact a little boy is in the hospital. I personally am hoping that I can be a mentor to this young man and show him a better life. I know you live what you know and I want to show him a better way." Lionel looked to Denise. "Now I'm not claiming to be any kind of a good person, that's for God himself to judge. I do think I am a better person than a man who beats up on a defenseless boy." Deinse turned her attention to the ranch house and noticed Tank standing at his door.

"I can tell you're a great man Lionel. I might have just met you, but I can tell."

"I sure hope so. Truth be told, I'm a little nervous about that boy. I was never really a kid person, but I can't help but care enough to bring him out here. Besides if his dad does find him, I have twenty men who will defend that kid without even meeting him." Denise agreed.

"Twenty men and a maid. Don't forget, my Uncle Joe taught me to shoot too. I may not be the best, but I can hold my own."

"That's good to know, you never know what kind of animal can make their way up to the house." When Tank made his way to the barn from his cottage, Denise followed his every step with her eyes. She didn't notice Lionel sitting with a smirk on his face watching her. "So you were saying?" Lionel pulled her out of her staring.

"What? Oh, um, what were you talking about?" Lionel laughed. "Stop laughing. I might not be ready to date again, but I can still notice a good looking cowboy."

"I never really thought about Tank being good looking, but whatever." Denise playfully slapped his chest.

"Even if I was interested, which I'm not, he probably thinks I'm off limits thanks to your little speech earlier. All the cowboys here probably think I'm a young child. Really Lionel, off limits? That's something you say about your younger sister." Both Lionel and Denise started to laugh about that. "I mean I know you meant well, but that was a little embarrassing."

"I'm so sorry. I didn't mean to embarrass you. I only want you to know that I would protect you. I care about all my employees but I won't put up with certain behaviors."

"If they do flirt with me are you really going to fire them?" Denise asked. She was shocked when he claimed that. Lionel looked at Denise so she could tell that what he was about to say was serious.

"My men are good men. However, they are men." They both kind of chuckled. "That being said, I'll always take care of my employees, both in the house and on the ranch. If you feel that any of my employees are acting inappropriately with you in any way, please come and talk to me. I saw the way you and Tank were introducing yourselves. I must say I've never seen Tank take to a person so easily. He's not much of a talker. So if you're asking about if I would fire Tank for flirting with you, no, I would never fire Tank. Tank's been on this ranch almost as long as I have. His father worked for my parents and Tank would come and hang out with his dad. I couldn't do half of what that man does on this ranch. Hell he is the ranch. Without him and Jim I'm not sure there would even be a ranch." Lionel patted Denise on the shoulder and excused himself to go to bed. Tomorrow was Friday and they finally got to meet Scott. They both went to bed with thoughts of the boy.

CHAPTER 3

Scott Wilson sat in the back of the black car as Maria got out and started to talk to Lionel. He didn't think much of the two story white farmhouse with a wrap-around porch. He just kept thinking about how long it might be until he had to go back to his parents. He knew his dad was going to be mad about him not coming home. Maria explained that he wouldn't be going home until his father was able to finish his court orders. Then she explained that she thought he would be safe with Mr. Lionel James on his ranch.

Maria came to the back seat of the car and removed his crutches. His left leg was broken, he had two cracked ribs, a sprained left hand and a bunch of bruises. He had to use crutches for a month, and his abs need to be wrapped tightly with an ace bandage for a few weeks. Mr. James walked over to help Scott out of the car.

"I got this old man. I don't need your help." Scott said and he immediately regretted his attitude. He knew this man had nothing to do with him being taken away from his dad. He just didn't want to get close and then be handed back to his dad. He knew a foster kid at school who was always being pulled back and forth between their parents and new foster homes.

"I know you got this son. I only wanted to help, but I'll stand back." Lionel took a step back, waited for Scott to stand up then held his hand out to him. "Name's Lionel James, but you can call me Lionel. I have got a room for you upstairs. Do you think you can handle the stairs? I can have my maid Denise trade you rooms until you are off the crutches." Scott looked at Lionel like he had to be joking. Why would he move his maid just so he didn't have to take the stairs?

"No, stairs are fine." Scott called as he started toward the house. "This ain't the first time I used crutches." Thinking he better behave, at least until Maria left, he called over his shoulder "Thank you." They continued into the house as Lionel grabbed the bag from the trunk.

"I think we are done here." Maria said. "You seem to have everything under control. I'll be in touch, but if you need me for anything in the meantime you have my number." Lionel confirmed as he helped her back into her car and watched her drive away. Lionel then turned back giving Scott his full attention.

"This is your house as long as you need a place to stay. Feel free to make yourself at home. I have cable, but it's not in your room yet. The cable company should be here Monday at the latest. I have Wi-Fi and a computer in my office that you're more than welcome to use. Do you have any questions?" When Scott only stared at Lionel he then continued to talk. "Okay boy, then follow me to your room." Lionel decided to go up the stairs first, but kept his eyes on Scott as he made his way up slowly. He stayed within arm's reach, in case he fell. At the top of the landing Lionel explained that the door on the right was a shared bathroom. The door on the left is Scott's room, and the door at the end of the hall was Lionel's. They made their way to Scott's room. "Go ahead and relax for a few minutes and get settled. We'll go shopping for some clothes and other stuff you may need. Once you are off those crutches, I'll expect you to pitch in around here. Have you ridden a horse before?"

"Of course I have never ridden a horse." Scott answered with an attitude. "I grew up in the city, not on some ranch in the middle of nowhere. Just so we're clear, I don't clean horse shit." Lionel just chuckled.

"We'll see boy, we'll see." They made small talk about what changes Scott wanted to do to his room and what things Lionel did expect. Scott didn't say much, just did a lot of agreeing. "Now even though Denise is the maid, you still need to keep your room clean." He pointed to the laundry basket. "You are to use this and not make Denise gather clothes from all over the room." Then they made their way to the kitchen where they met up with Denise.

"Hello, my name is Denise," she said as she pulled Scott into a hug. "Oh my goodness, did I hurt you. I'm so sorry." She jumped back when he stiffened and made a noise.

"It's alright." Scott told her. "Don't worry about it." Hugs weren't something he usually had a lot of, but he'd liked it. Denise was warm and smelled nice and something about her made him feel safe.

"I'll be doing the cooking and cleaning. If there's anything you like to eat, let me know so I can add it to the list before we go shopping."

"I really like any food." Scott replied with a smile. "I was lucky if I was able to eat a real meal once a week. Most of the time, I just had to eat whatever I could find around the house. But I do like Italian, like spaghetti and lasagna, but I don't like mushrooms." Denise smiled, already gathering ingredients to make spaghetti and meatballs for lunch. Lionel looked at Scott and shook his head.

"Boy, most kids your age always say pizza and hamburgers."

"I like those too, I just like Italian food better." Scott admitted. The three made small talk around the table; about food and what they liked to do for fun. Scott was having so much fun that he didn't even notice when he dropped the attitude. Then Lionel got up to go outside. Tank was the first person he saw.

"Tank, gather the men and meet me here in about ten minutes."

"How's the boy, Boss? I got a glimpse when he got out of the car, but couldn't make out much."

"Well, he's a scrawny little thing; that cast probably weighs more than he does. He was trying to have an attitude, but it doesn't fit the kid. For the last ten minutes while he was talking to Denise

and me he had already dropped it. He's a good boy. I can tell."
Tank gave Lionel a nod and then headed off to go collect the men.
Lionel went back into the kitchen to talk to Scott. "C'mon boy, we
have a meeting setup for you. I have a twenty man crew and they
will be responsible for your training while you're on the ranch. I
won't accept any attitude towards my men. Do you understand me
so far?" Lionel waited until Scott nodded. "You will do what they
tell you to do and you do it as soon as they tell you to do it. Do
you understand?" Scott looked at Lionel.

"Yeah, I hear you Old Man." Scott said as he tried to keep his
lips from smiling, but the top lifted up just a bit.

"Come on boy, let's go meet the crew." Scott and Lionel made
their way back outside and the introductions were started. Lionel
again told his crew to show Scott the way of the ranch and to be
respectful, as he was a city boy. "Tank, as soon as Scott is off these
crutches, you'll be teaching him how to ride. He has no experience
with horses since, as he said, he's a city boy." Lionel looked at Scott
to let him know that he was joking. "I think it's best if you start to
introduce him to horses while he's still on his walking sticks here.
What do you say Scott?" Scott was a little put off by Tank. He was
a huge guy and that was probably how he earned his name.

"Yes sir, that sounds good. I have only seen a horse in the
distance or on television." The crew all gave a small laugh. One of
the men called out.

"Don't be scared it only hurts when you fall off, or they kick
you off." The men again started to laugh but Tank stopped them.

"Shut up and don't scare the boy. Now introduce yourself
and get back to work." One by one the crew again introduced
themselves and headed back to work. Tank was the last person to
approach Scott.

"Name's Tank. I take my job and my horses very seriously.
They are gentle creatures and need respect. If you think you'll be
coming to my barn with an attitude and thinking you won't have
to do what I tell you, we will have a problem. I don't like problems.

However, you treat my horses with respect and you do what I tell you, we'll get along just fine. Do you get me boy?"

"Yes sir." Scott swallowed and answered.

"Don't call me sir. Name's Tank." Then he too left to go back to work. Tank noticed that Scott seemed to be scared of his size and thought he could use that to his benefit while the boy learned his way around the ranch. He didn't need to know that he was nothing but a teddy bear.

CHAPTER 4

"We should probably get going," Lionel said as he slapped his hand around Scott's shoulders. "We have to go to the ranch next door to pick up Rose, Denise's aunt. She's going to help us shop. I don't know about you, but I don't like to shop." Scott just shrugged his shoulders. He couldn't remember the last time he went shopping for anything. "So we'll get you some clothes and some things to keep you entertained until you're able to work." Scott was just staring at Lionel. No one had ever done anything so nice. Scott was sure there was a catch.

"Okay Old Man, what do I need to do in return?"

"I already told you. You'll be working my ranch while you're here. That being said, you need proper clothes and boots. As for the things to keep you entertained, that is just because I want to. Now are you ready?" Scott got a huge smile on his face.

"Yeah Old Man, lets go." Lionel thought he might hate being called an Old Man, but Scott made it sound more like respect than an insult, so he let it go. Lionel, Scott and Denise all jumped in the ranch truck and headed next door.

When they pulled up to the black iron fence that read J&R Ranch, Rose walked out to Lionel's truck and immediately introduced herself to him.

"Hello, my name is Rose. Why I'll be, look at you honey. Lionel didn't say you would be a looker. If you ever need anything, you just come on over. I'm also Denise's favorite aunt. My husband Joe is out of town right now or he would have come to introduce himself as well."

"I would get out so I could introduce myself properly, but with a cast on the leg it's kind of hard to get in and out of the truck. It's a pleasure to meet you Ma'am." Scott held his hand out to shake hers, but Rose just patted his chest.

"No, don't even bother honey. I can see you got a little banged up." Rose got in the back seat of the truck and sat next to Denise. The two started talking away about what they would do once they were in town. Rose had planned to start with the Wal-Mart, since they had almost everything in one store, and Denise intended to open a new bank account. They pulled up to Wal-Mart and got out. Denise went straight to the front where the bank was. Rose led the men to the clothing section. "You might be ten, but you sure are a tall creature. Do you know what size you wear?" She asked Scott. He just looked down at his shoes, ones that had seen better days, and replied.

"No, Ma'am, I just kind of wear whatever I can find and use this belt to hold them up."

"Well, a belt is a must. We'll get you some pants and shirts to fit as well as a couple of belts. Now let's see. First we need to find the size of your waist. Here try these pants on. They might be too long or too short, but that's okay. I'm looking to see the way they fit around your waist." Rose handed Scott three pairs of jeans to try on. "Now I want to see each pair, so come on out when you have them on." Rose yelled over the changing room door. Scott tried to get out of his pants, but with the room being small and the cast, it was harder than he thought.

"Um… is Old Man out there?"

"Right here boy, what do you need?" Lionel answered him.

"Um… I kinda need help with the cast and stuff." Lionel laughed quietly to himself.

"Okay boy, open up and let me in so I can help you." Scott opened the door and Lionel started to help him. As Lionel undressed Scott, he saw the bruising all over his back and sides. He didn't say anything and tried to hide the pity from his face. "Rose, this first pair is just too tight. Here I'll pass them over the door." The second pair was a little better, but still a bit too tight, so Lionel again passed them to Rose over the door. The third pair fit perfectly, except they were too long. Scott came out to show Rose just how long they were. She then went to get more pants to try on in different lengths. Finally he found some that fit him perfectly, both in the waist and the legs. Rose went and grabbed a couple of each color in that size. She also picked up a couple of sweat pants and some shorts for him to wear until the cast came off. Next they went to the shirts. He got a couple packages of the undershirts and when he was offered his choice of underwear he was stunned. He didn't know there were so many kinds. So Lionel threw a couple of each- briefs, boxers, and boxer briefs into his basket. "Try these out and whatever you like best we can come back and get more." Lionel told Scott. Next they headed to socks and Rose tossed in a few packages.

"Wait, I don't need so many. I can just wash my dirty socks." Scott tried to remove a couple of packages from the basket.

"No, once you start on the ranch you will need these. With the amount of work that we do, socks tend to not last so long. Trust me boy." Lionel responded and pushed the basket to the shoe department, where Denise met up with them.

"Okay, so do you know what size shoe you wear Scott," asked Rose.

"No Ma'am, again whatever I can get my hands on, I make due with." Rose smiled at Scott.

"Bless your sweet heart. We'll get you all fixed up and ready for the ranch in no time. Well then, let's get started." Rose found a shoe measuring device and took his measurements. "You'll need at least two different boots. So which ones do you like? I would suggest that you make sure they're not steel toed."

Scott walked up and down the aisle and he pointed to a pair that he could just pull on. He wasn't looking at the boots, but at the price. Lionel noticed what he was doing.

"These boots are going to hurt your feet by the end of the first day. You get what you pay for son. I'm not worried about the price. Let's look at these over here." Lionel walked him over to the more expensive section.

"I don't know Old Man. I won't be able to pay you back for all this. I know my dad won't pay you back when I have to go back to him. I would rather keep the price as low as possible."

"Son." Lionel started. "I'll be honest with you. I don't see you going back to your father; at least not for a while. I'm responsible for you while you live with me. I want to buy you these items. As for paying me back, I did tell you that you will be working on the ranch. So that being said, let's get you some good boots."

"I like these. Are they steel toed?" Lionel walked over and told him what a good choice these were. They found his size and he walked around again to find another pair, but these boots laced up. Lionel again told him what a good choice these were.

"Why not get a pair of shoes for the time you are relaxing and in the house." Lionel told Scott. So Scott walked up the aisle again looking for shoes and picked a pair. "Okay, now for the fun stuff." Lionel said as he rubbed his hands together. "Scott what do you like to do for fun?"

"I really didn't do anything. I mostly just did homework and tried to stay out of my dad's way." Everyone was quiet for a few moments.

"Okay, to the electronics department it is then." Lionel said in a loud cheery voice. He pushed his basket to the electronics section and found an employee. "Can you tell me what all the teens are into these days?" The employee gave Lionel the once over and started to walk to the game systems.

"Most teens have one of these systems, and then you just buy the game to go with it." The employee stated. "Which system do you have? I could help you pick out a game." Lionel explained that he just got custody of his nephew and they needed to start from scratch; so the employee talked to Scott and Lionel about each system. He explained what each system could and couldn't do. They looked at the games that went with each system and then Scott finally chose the PlayStation 3. Lionel allowed him to pick three games and some extra controllers. They got a couple of books to read as well and then, finally, they all headed to the front of the store to cash out. After loading the back of the truck, they headed back towards the ranch.

"How are you doing with that leg son? Do you feel up to one more stop?" Scott did hurt a little, but after the amount of money that Lionel just spent on him he wasn't about to stop him.

"I'm good Old Man, no worries. Let's go." So Lionel drove to Pop's Diner.

"As a thank you for all the help today ladies, please allow me to buy you dinner. Scott, they have some great food here, but I don't think they serve Italian." Everyone was excited and headed inside. Once they found their seat their waitress came over.

"Well, well, well, who do we have here?"

"Hey Trisha, this here is my nephew, Scott, and this is my new employee, Denise, who is also Rose's niece." Lionel made the introductions and they placed their order. "No one needs to know the real reason Scott is here." Lionel quietly explained to the table after Trisha had walked away, then looked at Scott. "If you're uncomfortable with that, we can make up a different story."

"No, I like the nephew idea. It's better than foster dad." Scott replied. After they ate, they went back to the ranch and everyone helped Scott carry his things to his room and set it all up. Rose left shortly after. Denise excused herself to finish the laundry she had started before they left. Lionel and Scott set up the PlayStation and played for hours. It was getting late, so Lionel was heading to bed.

"Hey Old Man, can I ask you something before you go?" Scott asked in an unsure voice.

"Of course son, anything and anytime."

"At the store you mentioned that you didn't think I would be going back to my dad. Do you really think that or did you just say it?" Lionel sat back down to get on Scott's level.

"I'll be honest with you. You might not always like what I say, but I will always be honest with you. You understand me." Scott shook his head in agreement. "I expect the same from your boy; honesty always, even if I don't like what you say." Scott promised him he would. "Good, now that we understand each other I can tell you, I don't know for sure what's going to happen. I will tell you that I called in a favor to have your dad prosecuted for what he did to you. It wasn't right to hurt someone so badly they ended up in the hospital. The fact that you're his son makes it so much worse. It's his job to protect you, not hurt you. When he gets out of jail I don't know if they will make you go back, but I promise you that I will fight for you. Realistically, I don't see you going back for a long time, if ever." They both quietly thought about what he just said. After a few minutes Lionel asked Scott how he was feeling.

"Honestly I'm not sure. I mean that's my dad. I don't want anything bad to happen to him, but at the same time, I'm glad he won't hurt me anymore. Then I think I should be sad he won't be around anymore, but I'm not."

"It's completely normal to feel the way you do. I would in your shoes." That seemed to settle Scott, having something in common with Lionel. "I'm going to go to bed now. If you need anything you know where I am." Scott acknowledged him and went to get comfortable in his bed. As Lionel went to turn off the light he reminded Scott. "Tomorrow you will be waking up at the same time as the ranch hands. I know you won't be working on the ranch, but you need to get your body ready for when you do. Good night boy."

"Night Old Man." Scott replied with a smile. That evening Scott laid in bed and thought about how nice Lionel was. He never asked for anything. When Scott would make a mistake, Lionel never yelled at him or tried to hit him. He wondered if it was bad to hope his dad never came for him.

*   *   *

Three months later and you would have thought Scott was born on the ranch. He was a natural at riding horses. Tank kept asking him if he was sure he never rode before. Scott learned to ride on Dreamer. However, soon after he learned, he found that he and Patches had a particular connection. It was almost time for school to start and Scott would have to go to a new school. He was kind of happy about that, but he was dreading having to explain everything to all his teachers. He was told that he would have the chores of feeding the horses and chickens before school; then he had to help in the field after school. He would be allowed to come in two hours before the other guys to do his homework. Until the school year started, his chores were to help with whatever needed to be done. Tank and Jim both made sure to teach Scott about all aspects of the ranch. Scott played his PlayStation every night with Lionel before bed. He learned to drive a ranch truck, but he wasn't allowed to leave the ranch yet. He had learned how to do most things on the ranch. Denise even taught him to cook some small dinners and how to wash his clothes properly. She and the ranch hands didn't have a problem teaching Scott anything since he was a fast learner, and he was thoroughly enjoying his new home.

CHAPTER 5

Seven years later, around Scott's seventeenth birthday, Lionel got a call from Maria. She explained that Scott's father had completed all necessary court ordered classes to regain custody of Scott.

"Are you serious? After all this time, he finally decides to be a dad." Lionel was beyond upset. "I can't believe this." Lionel was yelling, not necessarily at Maria, just at the situation itself.

"I understand your situation Mr. James, but please try to calm down." Maria told Lionel.

"Sorry, I'm just upset. I've come to love that boy as my own. He belongs on this ranch. What are my options? Do I have to allow him to go back?" Lionel was shooting off questions as they came to his mind.

"Mr. James, I understand that some time has passed and you have grown to care for Scott, but there's nothing that I can do at this point. I'm sorry. You will need to bring him to our offices no later than Friday by five." Maria apologized again and then hung up the phone.

Lionel sat at his desk trying to come up with some plan to keep Scott. Not knowing what else to do, he called his lawyer.

"I need to speak with Mr. Bradshaw as soon as possible." Lionel paused as Kyle's secretary spoke. "No, I will not wait. Tell him it's Lionel James on the phone." Kyle Bradshaw, his best friend and lawyer, picked up his end of the line as soon as his secretary told him who it was.

"Hey man, what is going on? How is it going out on the ranch? I heard yall got yourself a couple of pregnant mares." Kyle asked.

"Kyle, I'm sorry to be so curt with you, but I don't have time for idle chit chat right now. I need your help and I need it now."

Kyle finally heard the voice that Lionel was using and knew something was wrong. It took a lot for Lionel to lose his cool.

"Tell me Lionel. What is going on? How can I help?"

"Scott's piece of shit father; that's what's wrong. After seven years he finally decides he wants to be a part of Scott's life. I have to return Scott to him on Friday. I can't lose him, Kyle. He's like my own son." Lionel had to stop talking or he would break down in tears.

"I'm sorry my friend, honestly there is not much that can be done. If a judge orders him back, he has to go back. Let me look up something real quick, hold on." Lionel could hear Kyle typing away on his computer. "I was just looking for a loophole. Due to his age, he might be able to get an appointment with the judge. Then he can explain to the judge that he doesn't want to go back to his dad.".

Lionel thought about that for a minute. "Okay, make it happen. I have to go."

Lionel thanked his friend and hung up the phone. He walked up the stairs to Scott's room and looked around at how much that boy had come to be a part of his life. There was a picture of Scott and Lionel on his nightstand. Lionel was heartbroken, but before he did anything, he needed to talk to Scott. Lionel walked to the barn with the horses. Scott was always in the barn with the horses. He found him cleaning out the horse stalls and putting down clean hay.

"You know, I remember a smart mouth kid who once told me he wouldn't clean up horse shit." Scott looked over to Lionel and laughed.

"Yeah Old Man, but that smart mouth kid learned a lot about horses and taking care of them. So here I am." They both laughed, then Lionel got serious real quick.

"Hey Scott, son, I need to talk to you and this is serious. Come sit with me on the back porch and Denise will get us some tea." As they walked to the porch, Lionel was trying to think of how to approach this issue. "I have to tell you something Scott. Seven years ago I got a phone call. Child Protective Services needed a little ten year old boy to come stay with me. At that time, I was a lost soul. My wife had just left me. It wasn't until a few months after you came that I heard anything about her. That was through her lawyers letting me know that she wanted a divorce. I wasn't sure what to do with a young boy. I never had any kids. Ally and I tried but we were never able to conceive. After she left I just gave up looking for love. Then here comes a call about a boy who's had a hard life. I know what you went through all those years with your dad. I still get so fighting mad when I think about how he treated you. I tried to show you how good life can be."

"I'm really grateful for all that you've done. I have had a great life living here. I hate what my dad did, but it brought me here." Scott said. "I can see a different life than where I was headed. I don't even want to imagine where my life would be right now if it wasn't for you and this ranch."

"Scott, I got a call a little while ago." Lionel continued. "It was Maria from Child Protective Services explaining that your father has completed all his court mandated classes. He has made it known that he's ready for you to come live with him again." Lionel stopped talking to allow Scott time to process this.

"NO!!!" Scott shouted as he jumped off the porch and began pacing back and forth in front of it. "I won't go back to him. I don't care what classes he took or what he did. I'll never go back. I'm almost seventeen years old; they can't make me go back." Scott stopped yelling and looked up to where Lionel was still sitting. In almost a whisper, he asked. "Can they?" Lionel could see the fear in Scott's watery eyes. It made Lionel feel good that Scott wanted to stay here. He really loved Scott as his own son.

"I have to take you back to Child Protective Services on Friday. I have spoken to my lawyer. He said there's nothing *I* can do."

Scott lowered his head and began to sob. He loved it on this ranch. This ranch was his home. The only place he ever felt safe and like he could just be free. Scott started to think about the ranch. Who would take care of Patches? He needed to see his favorite horse. Scott stood to run to his stall, but before he could move Lionel grabbed him by his shoulder.

"Scott, I said there's nothing *I* can do." The way he said I let Scott know that this was not over.

"Wait! What do you mean nothing *you* can do? Is there something *I* can do?" Scott asked, getting hopeful.

"After Maria called and told me I have to send you back to your dad, I called my lawyer. Kyle said since your father completed all court requirements, there's nothing I can do. He looked into it a bit, and thinks with your age you could possibly talk to the judge about your case. You could try to explain your feelings and see how that goes, but there's no guarantee that the judge will let you stay." Scott started to look hopeless again. Lionel pulled Scott's face up to look right in his eyes. "Boy, let me tell you something, right here and now." Lionel stopped talking to make sure that Scott was looking him in the eyes as he said the next part. "You have come to be like a son to me. No matter what you choose to do or what the judge says, you will always have a place here. You turn eighteen in a little more than a year and then you can do as you please. Like I said, you will always have a place here. Do you hear me?" Lionel asked Scott to make sure he understood. With tears in his eyes, Scott gave Lionel a huge hug and said that he understood. With that conversation out of the way, both men went to Lionel's office to call Mr. Bradshaw.

Since Scott was due to be sent back to his dad on Friday, Kyle had already made an appointment with Judge Gomez for Thursday. Thursday morning Scott and Lionel went to town. Lionel took Scott to breakfast at Pop's Diner. They tried to act as if nothing was changing. They talked to other locals, and soon the men left to meet with the judge. After signing in and getting called to the judges chambers, Lionel explained his wishes. The judge asked Lionel to step out of the office so he could talk to Scott privately. After almost an hour of Lionel pacing up and down the hall, Scott and the judge came out. The judge agreed to allow Scott to stay on the ranch, but he had to stay with his father every other weekend until he turned eighteen. The judge explained that Scott was to try to give his father a chance, but that if his father abused him in any way; verbally, mentally or physically, then Scott was to report back to him immediately. Lionel couldn't hold in his excitement and grabbed Scott and gave him a long tight hug. Then he grabbed the judge's hand and shook it.

"Thank you so much. You don't know how much I love this kid. I know that it was supposed to be a temporary situation but I couldn't help but fall in love with him. Thank you again." Lionel was so excited.

Hearing Lionel tell the judge that he loved him made Scott tear up. He knew the Old Man cared about him, but to admit he loved him out loud, made Scott feel safe for the first time in his life. As they walked to the truck, Lionel threw the keys to Scott and told him to drive home. Home, Scott loved the sound of that. Once they got home, Scott went to his room to think. He really didn't want to go to his dad's, but since the judge allowed him to stay on the ranch, he would do it. Saturday morning he had to meet his father after seven years. He made up a bag to take with him and went to talk to his horse Patches.

CHAPTER 6

At the age of thirty two, Scott was thinking about settling down. He just didn't have any prospects in his town. He went out a few times. but most of the single women weren't marriage material. He thought about doing that online dating thing, but he thought that was more for losers. He worked all day and was too tired to party at night. Lionel and he had talked before bed every night since he came to live on the ranch. Scott took online courses and earned a degree in business management so he could help Lionel out in the office. Even though Lionel would deny it, he was getting up in age and didn't move around as easily as he used to. There was talk about selling the ranch at one time, but he had not heard much about it in years. Looking out over the acres of the ranch and feeling at peace, was what he loved most about it.

"Scott, there you are honey. Lionel wants to see you in his office." Denise delivered her message as she was walking towards the barn. Scott got up and noticed Mr. Bradshaw's car in the drive-way. He continued on to Lionel's office.

"You wanted to see me Old Man?" Scott had called Lionel Old Man since the day he came to stay with him. The first time he said it was with an attitude, but he continued just because he thought it was another name for father, though he never told Lionel that part.

"Kyle is here to help me out. I wanted you to hear about this from me now instead of later." Lionel explained. "I'm setting up my will. I know you heard the rumors of me selling the ranch. I did think about it, but this is your home. This land has been in my family for many generations. Since you have come to be like my son, I would like you to have it. I never had any children or I would have given it to them. You'll inherit the whole ranch." Scott's eyes got huge in surprise. He loved this ranch, but he didn't think Lionel would leave it all to him. Lionel smiled when he saw the shock on Scott's face. "There's a stipulation of course. The stipulation is you have to try to keep as many of the employees, as you can, for as long as you can. Many of them have been here longer than you have son, and it only seems right in my eyes that I take care of them as well." Scott was shocked at this news.

"Well... yeah I would take care of all these employees as you would have. Thanks Old Man, that means so much to me. Wow!" Scott walked around and gave Lionel a tight hug. Then they continued with the little things he wanted people to have and such. After Bradshaw left, Scott and Lionel talked out on the porch about what would happen when Scott took over the ranch. They went back and forth with ideas and changes.

*   *   *

A few months later, Lionel started to notice little things that needed to be done around the ranch. The paint was peeling and they had some loose boards here and there.

"Scott, I think we should start fixing up this old house. Look at how bad it's getting. I bet the inside is just as bad. Let's make a list of things that need to be done and start tomorrow. What do you say?" Scott brought up to Lionel that the front porch had a leak and the kitchen appliances also needed to be replaced. Lionel and Scott sat down and discussed what they both felt needed the most attention. Scott offered to pay for the repairs, but Lionel wouldn't hear of it. They made a list of supplies they would need to fix the roof and paint the house. Then they talked to Denise about what appliances she would like to see replaced. Scott and Lionel started taking measurements of everything they wanted to do.

Early the next morning Scott, Lionel, Tank and Denise took the truck to town and started to gather the materials needed for the projects. As the men headed to the building supplies, Denise went to the paint section of the hardware store. They had everything ordered, paid for and set up to be delivered to the ranch. The store said it would be there in about two hours. So they drove to the appliance store. Denise was in heaven. Lionel and Scott told her to pick out whatever she wanted. She picked out a dishwasher and a new stove. She also chose a refrigerator that had two doors and could hold about three times the amount of items she had now. Once she was done they set it up to be delivered the next day and they headed back to the ranch.

When they arrived at the ranch they noticed their supplies were already delivered. Denise headed inside to start lunch and call her Aunt Rose to tell her about the new appliances she would be getting.

Scott and Lionel and a couple of the ranch hands were on the roof tearing off the old shingles when Lionel slipped and fell off the roof. He landed on the ground hard and didn't move. Scott and the ranch hands hurried down the ladder to check on him. When Scott was about half way down he just jumped off the ladder and ran to Lionel. On the ground Lionel just laid there. It hurt to move and he couldn't catch his breath. Scott saw that he couldn't breathe so he ran inside to call 9-1-1.

"9-1-1 what is your emergency?"

"My father fell off the roof of a two story house. He can't breathe and it looks like he might have broken some bones. Please hurry." Scott hung up the phone after giving her the address and ran back to Lionel. Denise hurried outside to see if there was anything she could do to help. The ambulance was there within thirty minutes. Since they lived so far from town, it took them a little while to get there.

Tank had the ranch hands continue to remove the shingles. He then informed Jim of the deliveries that were scheduled for the next day. As they loaded Lionel in the back of the ambulance, Tank showed up with the truck. Tank had to physically pull Scott away from the ambulance and make him get in the truck. They followed the ambulance to the hospital. Once inside Scott and Tank ran to the nurse's station to get information.

"My father was brought in, please is he going to be alright?" Scott asked the nurse.

"What is your father's name sir?" The nurse asked him.

"Lionel. Lionel James." Scott answered almost out of breath.

"I'm sorry. I don't have any information at this time. I'll have a doctor come talk to you as soon as more information is available. Please have a seat over there in the waiting room." It was only about twenty minutes later, but it felt like hours, the doctor came into the waiting room.

"The family of Mr. James…" Scott shot up from his chair before the doctor could finish his sentence. "Sir, Mr. James took a pretty good beating from that fall. He has a broken leg and some minor bruising. The reason he was unable to catch his breath is that he has three broken ribs. It seems that one of those ribs punctured a lung and we will need to do surgery to fix that issue. As long as there are no complications during surgery, your father should be good to go in a few days. Do you have any questions? I really should be getting back to start on that surgery."

"No doctor, thank you. Please just keep us informed as much as you can." Scott replied. Tank pulled him away from the waiting room.

"Come on, it will probably be at least an hour. Let's get a drink and some food, then we come back and wait."

"No Tank, I need to wait here." Scott said.

"Boy, did you hear me ask a question? I didn't ask you if you wanted to; I said you are. Now let's go." Tank pulled Scott by the shoulders and walked him to the nurse's station. "Excuse us Ma'am. We are the family of Lionel James. We'll be in the cafeteria if anyone needs us or anything happens." The nurse just smiled and let them know that if anyone or anything happened she would call up to the cafeteria.

It was a long quiet ride to the cafeteria and Tank just kept his eye on Scott. Tank ordered each of them a cheese burger and fries and a soda. They found a quiet corner in the back.

"So, when did you start calling Lionel Dad?" Tank asked with a smile on his face. Scott just kind of shrugged his shoulders. He wanted to say since he was ten and came to live with Lionel, he'd always thought of him as a dad. "You know that man has loved you as if you were his own. When he told us some kid was going to be hanging around with us, he added the job of protecting you to our list of duties. Told us if we didn't like you hanging around us while we worked, we could find us a new job. Lucky for us you were a smart kid who learned fast. Now, there were times you got underfoot, but not many." Tank stopped talking trying to get him to talk back. "You remember that time you thought you could take that Betty girl out on horseback to the river and not get caught?" Both Tank and Scott laughed.

"Yes, I was young and she seemed happy enough to be alone. I didn't know that you guys were out riding the fence line. I almost had her all the way undressed by the time you guys rode up on us. I should have been mad at you guys, but lucky you stopped it when you did. How was I supposed to know Betty was a hooker?" Both of them laughed again. They just kept talking about past memories. Scott couldn't believe how fast time flew by. They had been eating and talking for a little over forty five minutes. They made their way back to the elevator and went to the waiting room. When they got there the doctor was just coming out of the door. He didn't look too good, he looked tired and stressed. Scott grabbed onto Tank for some kind of support.

"The surgery was a success. Mr. James is able to breathe on his own and his leg is in a cast." Scott let out a breath he didn't even know he was holding.

"That's great! Can we go see him now?" Scott asked. The doctor gave Scott a look that indicated there was more to be said.

"You may want to sit down for this son. I'm sorry to have to tell you this. As we were operating to repair his lung we found cancer cysts. I'm sorry. If we would have found them sooner we might have been able to do something, but… I'm so sorry."

"What are you saying? Are you saying he has cancer and is dying?" Scott gave the doctor a look that said he didn't believe him. "No!!! He's a strong man and he would have told me if he was sick." Scott fell to the floor. Tank picked him up and set him in a chair and just held him.

"Look Scott, man up, he needs you now more than ever. When you really needed him he was there. Now it's time to repay him and be there for him. Take a few minutes to catch your breath. Then, you will go in there and be supportive and tell him how we are going to fight this thing. Do you get me boy?" Tank let Scott know there was no turning back. After a few minutes of Scott getting his emotions in check, both men walked into Lionel's hospital room.

"Hey Old Man, if you wanted to take a break just say so next time. No reason to go break a leg and a rib." Scott joked with Lionel. Lionel tried to keep things light as well and pretend that he would be going home soon.

"Scott I need you to go back to the ranch. I need the old appliances out of the kitchen so that they can bring the new ones tomorrow. I'll be fine. They have me on so many pain killers I won't be able to talk much anyway. Go on home, and come back tomorrow. Tank, help him. Now I'm tired, so I'll see you boys tomorrow." Lionel told the guys. Scott walked to the nurse's desk and left his and Tank's phone numbers as well as the house number in case anything happened.

At the house Scott and Tank found Denise sitting in the living room crying.

"How is he? Please tell me he's alright." Denise practically begged.

Tank grabbed Denise and held her in a hug. "I'm sorry we should have called sooner, he did survive the fall. He has a broken leg and three broken ribs. One of the ribs punctured his lung, but the doctors were able to save him. However, when they had him open to repair the lung, they found cancer and it's so bad there's nothing they can do." Scott's eyes filled with tears as Tank filled Denise in. Denise broke down and Tank told Scott he was going to take her to her room.

"The appliances will be here tomorrow so I need to clear out the old ones. Do you have it all ready to be moved?" Scott asked Denise.

"Yes, I took all the extra food that needed to be cold to the ranch house fridge and I have everything else ready to go." As Tank walked Denise to her room, Scott didn't wait for him to help him. He went to the kitchen, unhooked the gas lines from the stove and moved it outside. When he went back inside there was an envelope on the floor where the stove had been; it was yellow and dusty. Scott picked it up and read the name Allison Lahey on the return address label. Wasn't that Lionel's ex-wife's name? It didn't look open but the post date was from over twenty years ago. That was around the time he came to live with Lionel. Not sure what to do with it, he decided to open the letter. Scott sat outside and opened the letter and pulled out the contents. First thing that fell out was a picture of a sonogram. Then Scott read the letter.

Dear Lionel,

I know you are probably wondering why I'm writing. I guess you are still wondering why I left you. I want to apologize for how this came about. I need you to know that I have loved you with all my heart. I still love you with all my heart. I'm so sorry. I just couldn't live on that ranch any longer. I'm a city girl, born and raised. I tried so hard to live that country life. I just wasn't cut out for it. I just couldn't do it anymore. I know that if I told you how I felt you would have given up on your dreams. I couldn't let you give up your family legacy for me. Or you would have tried to talk me into staying and I probably would have. If I stayed I would have started to resent the land, or worst of all…you. I love you too much for that. However, I have something I should have told you. I did not tell the lawyers about this so it was not in the divorce papers. I have thought about not telling you at all, but I think you should at least know. When I left you, I was two months pregnant. I didn't know until after I left. I thought about coming home many times. However, I don't want to raise a child on the ranch. I'm so sorry. You should know that I'm due in May. It's a girl and I'm going to name her Bobbie Jean. I love you and thought you would want to know.

I love you Always,
Ally

Scott stared at the letter for what felt like hours. Should he tell Lionel he had a daughter? Should he act like he had never seen it? He went into the office to see if he could find any information. He wanted to see if he could find anything out before he said anything. Scott turned to the internet and typed in Allison Lahey and found three possible matches. One woman lived in New York, one in Indiana and one that passed away four years ago. Looking up the two living women, he knew they were not the same woman he was looking for. He started to look at the Allison that passed away. It seems she was sick for a while. Her obituary listed a daughter named Bobbie Lahey. So he typed in Bobbie Lahey and found a Facebook page. Her page listed her as living in Colorado. It however, did not have a photo. Damn it!! Now what should he do? He called Tank into the office.

"What do you know about Allison James?" Tank looked at Scott like he was crazy.

"I knew her as a sweet person who just didn't belong in the country. It's not for everyone. Why are you asking? I hope you're not going to try to track her down since Lionel is sick. I don't think that's a good idea." Scott just sat back and handed Tank the letter. Once Tank looked back up, Scott showed him everything he found out so far.

"What should I do?" Scott asked Tank.

"I think you should fly to Colorado and bring her back." Tank advised. So Scott made his plane reservation for the first available flight the next day and packed a bag.

The next morning Tank was already at the house. Denise was serving him breakfast and when she saw Scott, she made him a plate too. Scott and Tank talked about possibilities of what could happen. They planned for if she did come back to Texas and if she didn't come back.

"I am just saying, I wouldn't tell Lionel just yet. What if she chooses not to come back? If she does come back, then we can find a way to break it Lionel." Tank told Scott. They both agreed not to tell Lionel about her unless she came back with him. Tank took Scott back to the hospital for a quick visit with Lionel before he drove him to the airport. Scott had about thirty minutes before his flight was to leave. As he was waiting for takeoff he started to think about how crazy all this was. He was hoping her Facebook page was up to date. It said she worked at the local bowling alley so that is where he was going to try first. If she didn't still work there he was hoping they could help him find her.

CHAPTER 7

Bobbie Lahey was dog tired after her shift at the restaurant and wanted nothing more than to take a long hot shower and go to bed. However, that wasn't going to happen. She still needed to go to her shift at the bowling alley. Bobbie worked mornings at the restaurant and then evenings at the bowling alley. Sometimes if she had a night off she would hang out with Lynn Daniels, her best friend since elementary school. She owed that girl for so much. It was hard to grow up with a single mother. She never knew her dad. Her mother even kept his name a secret and never talked about him. Bobbie's mother, Allison, told her that her father knew about her and that he didn't want anything to do with her. Because of that it had been just the two of them, but Lynn had always been there for her.

Just as she let herself into her tiny one bedroom apartment, the phone rang. As she was running to the phone she tripped over the rug. Her purse fell and most of the contents spilled out. Luckily she was able to stop herself from falling, but twisted her ankle and stumped her toe in the process. By the time she made it to the phone she was just in time to hear the other end of the line hang up. Great, she thought, what else could go wrong today. She looked at her once white shirt that was covered in ketchup, jelly, syrup, and some other unidentifiable stain and felt overwhelmed.

She had lived with her mother in a three bedroom two story house, until her mother passed away four years ago. She had a long painful battle with breast cancer. For the last four years, Bobbie had been working to pay off her medical bills. It seemed the more she paid off, the higher the balance got. They already sold the house and most of the items inside, but that barely made a dent in the amount of medical bills. She worked two jobs and barely had enough to pay the rent and get food. Good thing the restaurant and bowling alley fed the employees for free. Bobbie took a deep breath and went to rinse off in the shower. She would barely have time to change into the bowling alley uniform and get to work. Both the restaurant and bowling alley were within walking distance of her apartment. That cut down on a car payment, gas, and car insurance; not to mention maintenance repairs. Bobbie ran the few blocks to the bowling alley and clocked in five minutes early. She went to get her station ready for the day. Since it was a Tuesday she would probably be in the front desk. That was her least favorite station. She preferred the snack section instead. Maybe she could trade with someone. As she was walking over to the snack station to ask if someone wanted to change stations, she walked right into a customer.

"Oh my, I'm so sorry. I wasn't looking at where I was going. I'm so sorry." Bobbie apologized to the customer."

"It's alright. I was looking around instead of where I was going. I do apologize. I was looking for an employee."

"Oh, maybe I can help you. Who are you looking for?" Scott rubbed his hands across his face, which he did when he was nervous.

"Actually I'm not sure she still works here, or if she even did. I'm looking for a girl named Bobbie." Bobbie couldn't move or make a sound. She had never seen this guy before in her life. She was sure a man with those eyes and those muscles would be unforgettable.

"Um… can I ask what you need her for? I mean is this professional or personal?" Scott smiled.

"If you can just point me to her..." Scott started to say but Bobbie cut him off.

"Um... can you wait over at that table for a few minutes?" Bobbie went behind the snack bar to talk to Layla and see if she could switch stations for the night. Layla jumped on the opportunity. She hated the smell of the food after work. Then Bobbie walked over to Brad who was also working the snack section. "Hey Brad, I just switched stations so I'll be working with you."

"Cool, better than Layla complaining all night." They both shook their heads knowingly. Layla complained about everything.

"Hey, there's a guy asking to see me. I've never met him before, but I'll be talking to him over at that table. If you get too busy just let me know." Bobbie said.

"What do you mean you don't know him?" Bobbie explained the interaction that happened a few minutes ago.

"He asked me if I knew Bobbie. I'm pretty sure this guy doesn't know me either." Brad was not happy and told her to be careful.

"Don't go anywhere but to that table, I'm going to be watching you. If you take the ponytail out of her hair, that means you need me to come rescue you." Brad informed her as he looked at the man at the table. Bobbie started laughing.

"Thanks Brad. I'll be sure to stay at that table, so let me know if you get busy."

"So you wanted to talk to me?" Bobbie asked Scott as she walked to the table. Scott took a moment to really look at her and could see the resemblance to Lionel. They had the same eyes, nose, and hair color. Not knowing how to bring this up Scott said two words to Bobbie to test the waters.

"Lionel James." Bobbie stared at Scott like he lost his mind.

"Sorry I have no idea what or who you're talking about." That's what Scott was afraid of. He slowly pulled the envelope out of his pocket and set it on the table. Bobbie opened the envelope and a sonogram picture fell out. She looked at the picture and saw her mother's name. She then opened the letter and read it. She read it a second time and when she looked back at Scott she had tears in her eyes. "I don't understand." Bobbie tried to put the picture and the letter back in the envelope but her hands were shaking too bad. Scott took them from her and placed the letter and picture back in the envelope and put it back in his pocket.

"We were redoing the kitchen appliances in the house. I moved the stove and found this letter. Lionel has never seen it. I opened it, and I tracked you down, all without Lionel knowing. The thing is, Lionel is in the hospital and he probably won't live much longer. I thought if I could find you and take you to him..." Bobbie interrupted him.

"I'm sorry. Are you my brother or something?" Scott laughed.

"No, I was taken in and raised by Lionel when I was about ten and I just never left that ranch. I do see Lionel as my father, but no we aren't related. Lionel will be so happy to meet you. So go talk to your boss and tell him you need time off for a family emergency, then we can fly out tonight."

"WHAT?" Bobbie didn't realize she was screaming until Brad walked over to check on her.

"Is everything alright here?"

"Yes, sorry Brad. Can you give me a few more minutes then I'll be there to help you?" Brad walked away and Scott gave her a dirty look.

"Look, Bobbie you don't understand, Lionel will probably not last too much longer. I took a chance on you when I could have been spending my time with him. He's a great man and a great dad. I'm sorry that life ended up how it did. The end story is he never knew about you. I'm leaving to go back to Texas. I'll be leaving a ticket in your name if you choose to come. I'm sorry to drop this on you then leave, but I have to get back before it's too late. Thank you for your time." Scott got up and left. Bobbie sat there in a stunned state until Brad walked over and asked if she was okay.

"That guy knows my dad. I don't even know my dad. He had a letter from my mom." Bobbie looked up to Brad with watery eyes. "What do I do Brad? That guy says my dad is dying and he never knew about me. My mom said she told him and he wanted nothing to do with me. I'm so confused." Brad gave Bobbie a hug.

"Go tell the manager something came up and you need a few days off starting immediately. Then you need to talk to the restaurant and tell them the same thing. Then you need to go get that plane ticket I heard him tell you about and meet your dad. You will always wonder. You need to do this Bobbie." Bobbie hugged Brad back and walked to the manager's office. The manager was super cool most of the time. After she explained the situation, the manager agreed that she needed to fly to Texas to see her dad.

"Go, you will have a place to work when you get back. Just please be careful." Bobbie left the bowling alley and walked home. She immediately called Lynn to come over.

"Lynn, girl you need to come over here. I mean NOW!!" Within ten minutes, Lynn was opening the door to Bobbie's apartment. Bobbie was sitting on the couch with watery eyes staring out the window when Lynn walked over to her. Lynn didn't ask what was wrong, she just grabbed her in a tight hug. After a few minutes Bobbie explained what happened and Lynn just stared at her.

"You mean he never even knew about you? What are you going to do?" Lynn asked.

"I talked to both of my managers and both agreed I should go to Texas. I think I'm going to go to Texas." Bobbie said.

"Well then let's get you packed up and call about that ticket." Lynn told Bobbie as she started to walk to her bedroom. "You said he has a ranch. I bet he has some good looking cowboys on that ranch. Not that this is the time, but I'm jealous of you. I want to see some cute cowboy butts." Lynn said jokingly to try to cheer up Bobbie.

"Well Scott - the guy that came tonight - was sort of cute. Maybe you should come with me." Bobbie added. Lynn stopped what she was doing. Bobbie always downplayed the cute guys.

"I really wish I could. I have a very important meeting tomorrow or I would. Maybe I could…"

"No. Don't change anything for me. I think I need to do this on my own. But thank you." Bobbie stopped her, she knew that Lynn would drop everything and be there if she really wanted her to.

"Okay." Lynn got a smile on her face "So when you say kind of cute do you mean he was cute or…" Laughing Bobbie answered.

"Fine, if you must know he was hot as hell and if all the cowboys are like him in Texas, I may never come back." Both girls started to laugh and make more jokes as they packed up pants and the only pair of boots that Bobbie owned. Lynn called the airport and checked on that ticket, she was able to set up a flight for early the next morning.

"Okay, I'll drive you to the airport tomorrow, but we have to leave at like butt early in the morning, so I'm just going to sleep over."

After showering and getting everything ready, both climbed in Bobbie's queen sized bed and fell asleep. Lynn was not joking when she said they needed to be up early; at three in the morning her alarm went off.

"Oh my god. Today's the day. Get up lazy bones. Today you go meet your dad. Girl, today is Texas day. Get up." Lynn was in a rare good mood this early. Bobbie finally rolled over.

"Ugh, why are you happy? Come back to bed. We can do Texas another day." Lynn used her feet to push Bobbie out of the bed. Bobbie hit the floor hard. "Did you just push me out of bed, with your nasty feet?" Lynn could not say anything because she was laughing so hard. Finally catching her breath she called out.

"Oh my god. That was way easier when we were teenagers. How much do you weigh now? Damn girl, lay off the cookies." Bobbie stood up and threw the pillow toward Lynn.

"Bitch get a pedicure once in a while. I think you cut my skin open with those toes." Lynn stopped laughing.

"Are you talking about my toes? You have no room to talk, smelling like a squashed banana." Lynn called back. Bobbie just looked at her.

"Did you just call me a squashed banana?" Lynn had no come back.

"Look it's too early in the fucking morning for this. Just go take a damn shower and I'll make you something to eat."

"A squashed banana. Really?" Bobbie said, shaking her head as she started towards the shower.

Once Bobbie got out of the shower, they were both more awake. Lynn went over the plan as they ate.

"I am going to take you to the airport then go home and catch up on some sleep. I'll let my dad know what's going on, so he might be calling you. Now eat up, we don't want to be late."

Bobbie nodded and did as she was told. When they finished, they loaded Bobbie's bags into the back of Lynn's car and headed to the airport. The car was full of nervous energy, but neither girl spoke. As soon as they parked and got out of the car, Lynn pulled Bobbie into a hug.

"I really wish I could do this with you, but I can't. Let's go make sure you have a ticket before I leave." Lynn and Bobbie made it to the ticket counter and Bobbie told the attendant that she should have a ticket waiting for her. The ticket lady confirmed she did and wished her a wonderful flight. The girls only had a couple of minutes before Bobbie had to board the plan. "Here, it's not much, but you might need some cash for a taxi or something." Lynn offered money to Bobbie.

"I can't take that." Bobbie tried to decline, but Lynn stuffed it into her purse and walked away.

"I love you Bobbie. Be careful and call me often." Lynn waved then turned and headed to the parking garage.

Bobbie was in her seat and thinking maybe this wasn't such a good idea after all. Maybe her dad wouldn't want to see her. Did this Scott guy think of that? What she didn't think about was a place to stay once she landed. The flight was about two hours. The woman next to Bobbie kept talking about her marriage problems. Bobbie just smiled and pretended to be interested. She was too distracted to make out much; something about sleeping with men in other states not counting as cheating. Once the plane landed Bobbie looked in her purse for her cell phone. She saw the money that Lynn pushed in there, fifteen hundred dollars. I can't believe that girl, she thought. Well yeah, she could. Lynn didn't have money trouble. She was always trying to take care of Bobbie.

It wasn't until then that Bobbie realized she had no idea what hospital her father was in, and that she hadn't gotten Scott's number. Damn, how crazy am I to just jump on a plane because some strange guy told me to? Bobbie thought to herself. She sat in one of the chairs and pulled up the Google app on her phone and typed in hospitals near me. She tried each one, asking if her father was a patient. On the third try she told the receptionist that her father, Lionel James, might be a patient and needed to know his room number. A few minutes later, the lady on the phone told her he was in room seven thirty four. Good, she knew what hospital, now she needed to find a ride. Walking outside she hailed a taxi. Thirty minutes later, she was pulling up to the hospital and paid the driver. She walked inside, but instead of heading straight to his room, she sat in one of the chairs in the lobby. She was trying to get her emotions in check. She couldn't believe that just last night a stranger told her that he knew her father. Then he said she needed to come with him right away, when she refused he got mad and told her a ticket would be waiting for her at the airport. Then she actually got on a plane and flew to Texas, where she didn't know anyone. Again, she thought that maybe this was a bad idea. She called Lynn and Lynn gave her a pep talk.

"Look Bobbie, you made the hardest step. You got on that plane. Now you're so close to the one person, who your whole life, you have always wanted to know about. Go talk to the man and see what he has to say. I'll be here for you. Always!" Lynn hung up the phone before Bobbie could use her to back out.

So Bobbie did the only thing she could do, she headed to the elevators and pushed the button for the seventh floor. Once the elevator stopped, she took a deep breath and walked toward room seven thirty four. Before she walked in the room she took one more deep breath. Pushing the door open, she walked right into Scott again.

"We need to quit meeting like this." Scott joked with her. He pulled her out of the room before she could even get a look at her dad. "I'm sorry. I pulled you out because I didn't think you were coming, so I didn't tell Lionel about you, just a fair warning, okay." Bobbie shook her head as she understood. They both walked back into the room. "Hey Old Man, glad you are laying down. I have some news for you. Hope you have that oxygen ready. You're going to need it." Scott tried to keep the mood light.

"Well boy, I see you got yourself a pretty little thing here, guess you're getting married and leaving me." Bobbie blushed at the fact that her dad thought she was pretty. All these years wondering if her father ever thought about her, only to learn he didn't even know about her. The first thing he thought was that she was pretty. Scott laughed then he looked at Bobbie and agreed with how pretty she was. She looked even better blushing.

"Now come on Old Man, do you really think you can get rid of me that easily?" Both men chuckled. "Okay look, I have to tell you something and this is serious. If we were home we would be on the back porch and have Denise bring us some tea." That is how they usually shared the important news, so that got Lionel's attention causing him to sit up straighter. "I'm sorry for not telling you before, but I had to make sure. I hope you understand." With those words, Scott pulled out the envelope from his pocket. "I found this when I removed the stove a couple days ago." Scott handed Lionel the envelope and stepped back to give him as much privacy as he could.

Bobbie was now sitting in a chair pulled away from her father. She took this time to really look at him. Her eyes teared up when she noticed all their similarities; the eyes, the nose, even the hair color. Lionel opened the envelope and that same sonogram picture fell out. He stared at that picture with his ex-wife's name and, noting the date, his eyes got watery. He looked at the picture and then at Bobbie. Bobbie nodded her head to let him know that was her in the sonogram picture. With more tears running down his face Lionel started to read the letter. When he was done, he was in full tears. He reached out for Bobbie who jumped to hug him too.

"I'm so sorry baby, I didn't know. I swear, if I knew I would have come after you. I'm so sorry." Lionel kept repeating that over and over. Bobbie hugged him and told him that it was alright; that she understood. A throat cleared and they both looked at Scott.

"I hope you can understand why I didn't tell you right away." Scott tried to explain to Lionel. "I went to find Bobbie first, to see if she was up to meeting you. I didn't want to tell you and then have her not want to meet you. I wasn't sure what she knew about you or if she even knew about you. From what I gathered while in Colorado, she didn't know anything." Scott made sure he basically updated each of them with how the story fell together. He explained that they were working on the house and Lionel took a fall which was why he's in the hospital. Then he explained how he found the letter under the stove and opened it. He told Lionel what his meeting was like in Colorado and how he managed to find Bobbie. "Now if both of you will excuse me, I need to get a drink. Bobbie, would you like something from the cafeteria?" Scott asked as he was heading that way to give them some time alone.

"No thank you Scott." Scott left and the two started to talk.

"You're so beautiful, just like your momma. I bet you have many questions for me since I know I have so many for you." They were both just staring at each other, smiling with tears in their eyes. Lionel decided to go first. "Let me tell you about my life. Your mom and I were married. Then your momma just up and left me one day." Bobbie was surprised and let out a little gasp, but Lionel just shook his head. "I made a trip to town and when I got back she was gone. It took me some time to get myself back on track. I had a neighbor that was very helpful. Rose made sure I had food at night and she would try to do some cleaning, but with her own house needing tended to; it got pretty bad. Then about a month after your mom took off, I got a call from Child Protective Services telling me that they had a little boy who needed a home. At first I turned them down until they explained that he would be released from the hospital a couple days later from a beating his dad gave him. So I couldn't turn him away. That boy, Scott, he ended up saving me. I have grown to see him as my own child since I didn't know I had any. I swear Bobbie, if I had any idea at all, I would have hunted your momma down."

"I can tell how much Scott loves you. For him to go to Colorado to track me down - a virtual stranger - when he found the note. Then he kept all that a secret, in case I wasn't going to show. I won't speak badly about my momma. However, she did tell me that she told you and you wanted nothing to do with me. She didn't put your name on my birth certificate or I would have tried to track you down. I have always wanted to meet you. I just didn't know how. When I would ask mom about you she would get defensive. Later on she got really sick with breast cancer and I had to take care of her. About four years ago she lost her battle." Lionel's machines started to beep loudly, stopping Bobbie from continuing her story. The nurses came rushing in and made Bobbie wait in the waiting room. As soon as she got there she called Scott to let him know. "His monitor started to beep so they made me leave. I'm in the waiting room now." Bobbie was telling him.

"I'm on my way back." Before he could finish the nurse was already calling her back in.

"Sorry it was only a precaution. You can come back in now." When Bobbie walked back in Lionel was explaining that he was fine.

"I'm just a little broken-hearted. I'll be fine. I'm sorry for worrying all of you." The nurse double checked his vitals again and warmed him to try to stay calm. He took Bobbie's hand and asked her to continue.

"I don't even know where I was going with my story."

"I'm sorry sweet girl, you had explained that Ally fought cancer. Go from there."

"Ok. um since then I have been working as a waitress in a restaurant during the day and at night I work in a bowling alley." Bobbie tried to talk about herself, even though it wasn't in her nature. Scott walked in with a plate of eggs and bacon and handed them to Bobbie.

"I know you took an early flight to be able to be here this early, so here, eat up. You're going to need lots of energy to hang with this Old Man." Bobbie reached for the plate and thanked Scott. "You're welcome to stay at the ranch while you're here. Is that something you would be comfortable with?" Bobbie gave a shy smile and nodded in agreement. "So do you have hotel reservations I need to cancel?" Scott asked Bobbie. Bobbie shook her head.

"When you left, you just left. You told me about a ticket you left for me and that was it. Once I landed, I realized that I didn't know anything. You told me his name and that he was in a hospital, but you never said which one. So I just started to call all the hospitals and on the third try I got this place. Then I caught a cab and here I'm. I figured once I met my dad I would worry about a place to sleep."

"Oh shit! I'm so sorry, I didn't realize that I didn't give you any information before I left. I'm so sorry. I was in a hurry to get back. Do you have a phone? Let me give you my number before I forget in case something else happens." Scott exchanged numbers with Bobbie.

"You are such a fool boy. I raised you better than that." Lionel joked with Scott as he hit him across the back of his head. That got Bobbie laughing. Hearing Bobbie laugh did something to Scott. He wanted to hear that again.

"Tell me Old Man, is that the lesson you taught me when you took Rose and Denise to town then left them there because you forgot they rode with you?" Scott asked in a joking manner. Bobbie laughed.

"You didn't leave two women stranded, did you?" She asked in horror.

"Well they were taking so long shopping; I guess I kind of forgot they came along." Lionel laughed along with the others.

"I'll call Denise and let her know we have a house guest. I'll put her up in your room until you come home." Scott told Lionel. Just then the phone rang and Bobbie reached into her purse.

"Hello? Hey Lynn."

"I wanted to make sure you actually met your dad and didn't chicken out. I wish I could have gone with you."

"Yeah, I made it to his room safely. Yes, I did get to meet him and he's pretty cool, you would love him. Actually I'm in his room talking to him right now."

"Oh my God! Is he nice? What does he look like? Do you look like him? Did you ask him any of the questions you've had all these years? Are all the cowboys on his ranch cute? Why are you not answering me?"

"If you would be quiet for a minute I would try to answer you. He really didn't know about me. We are both kind of still in shock about meeting each other. I haven't been to the ranch so I can't tell you about that."

"Is that cute cowboy that came here in the room too? Tell me in great detail what he looks like. Does he have on those tight pants that really highlight the bulge?" Bobbie was blushing while talking to Lynn, making Scott curious as to what was being said on the other end of that line.

"Put your other dad on the phone. I want to talk to him." Bobbie was not sure what would come out of her mouth, so she hesitated to hand the phone over to Lionel.

"Okay hold on." Bobbie covered the phone with one hand and looked toward Lionel. "My friend wants to talk to you, but if you're not up for it, I'll have her call later." Lionel was reaching for the phone as Bobbie finished her sentence. "Before I give you the phone, I must apologize in advance. She was born without a filter." Bobbie slowly passed Lionel the phone.

"Hello? Yeah this is Lionel."

"Are you sure she's your daughter? I mean some strange man comes and tells her to come visit but how do I know she is your daughter?"

"Yes, she's my daughter. Just look at the two of us and you can tell."

"I'll have her send me a picture of the two of you. I think I need to come down to Texas to make sure though. I mean I also need to see for myself how sexy those Texas cowboys really are."

"I would love to have you over to the ranch when you get a chance." Laughing at the next part, he answered Lynn. "I'm not sure if my cowboys are sexy or not. I don't hire them based on looks. I can tell you that I have heard many women talk about how hot my boy Scott is." Bobbie was beet red with embarrassment since she knew what Lynn was asking on the phone.

"Is your Scott the one that came to Colorado? Is he taken. You know married, single, gay?"

"No, I don't believe my Scotty is not taken. Are you single Scott? Inquiring minds want to know." Lionel pointed to the phone as proof about the wanting to know part. He was quiet as he waited for Scott's answer. Scott looked at Bobbie.

"Yes I'm single, but I'm thinking about settling down." That look didn't get past Lionel and he answered Lynn.

"Yup, he's single, but if he had his way I think he would be staking claim to my lovely daughter here." Both Bobbie and Scott looked at Lionel with their mouths open. Lionel just started to laugh harder, as well as Lynn on the line. A knock came at the door. "Okay Lynn, looks like my nurse is here so I'll chat with you later. Okay, bye." Lionel hung up and handed the phone back to Bobbie. The nurse walked in and explained that he needed to be taken for some more tests.

"It will probably take a while and by the time he's done visiting hours will be over. So you might want to say your goodbyes now." Bobbie leaned over and gave her dad a hug.

"First, I am sorry for whatever she said. I probably don't want to know. I'll see you tomorrow, okay?" Lionel squeezed her tighter.

"I like her. She is a great friend to have. She will keep anyone on their toes. I'll be looking forward to morning when I get to see you again. My beautiful daughter." Lionel gave her a kiss on the cheek and a hug.

"I'll be bringing her back early in the morning so you better be ready Old Man." Scott walked over and hugged Lionel. So low that Bobbie could not hear, Lionel whispered in Scott's ear. "You better respect my girl."

CHAPTER 8

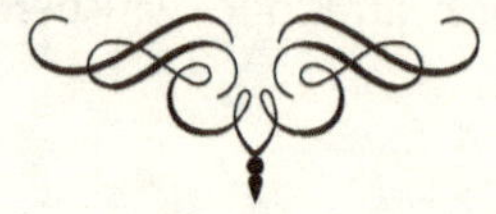

Scott took Bobbie to the ranch. Along the way he pointed out different places of interest.

"This is the diner that your dad always stops at when he comes to town. It is actually where your parents met. We can come back sometime and I will show you his booth."

"That's cool. It's sad that you know more about my parents history than I do." Scott was quiet for a minute.

"I'm sorry. This must be so hard on you."

"It's okay. I mean, yeah I'm still trying to get my head around the fact that I met my dad but I'm okay." A few minutes later Scott continued to point out special places.

"This is the hardware store that he prefers over the one across town. And this is the high school I graduated from." He looked over at her as they pulled up to the ranch "So have you ever ridden a horse?"

"Nope." She shook her head. "We always lived in the city and there's no place to ride there." Bobbie replied.

"That's cool, we have plenty if you'd like to learn. I didn't ride my first horse until I came to the ranch. Tank taught me, but I can teach you." Scott offered. They walked into the house and he showed her to Lionel's room. "This will be your room until your father comes home. In the meantime I'll have Denise start to get the guest room cleared out. It has become our room to store all things."

"This room will be fine, thanks." Bobbie replied as she entered her father's room and Scott turned to leave. She started to look around at the pictures on his dresser. There was a picture of her mom and dad when they were younger. She held the picture and sat on the bed. She wondered what it would have been like if her parents had stayed together and she was raised on this ranch. Once her feet hit the ground, she felt at home here. Lost in thought, she was spooked by the knock on the door.

"Hey I have to ride the fence line to make sure there are no issues. Would you like to ride along with me?" Scott asked. Bobbie looked at him and blushed.

"I have never been around a horse before and I'm kind of scared."

"No problem, meet me downstairs in five minutes and I'll have Tex ready. You can ride with me tonight and Tank and I can start to train you tomorrow to ride your own horse. Tank is a great trainer, he taught me everything I know about horses." Bobbie just shook her head in agreement and Scott walked away.

Downstairs she saw him walking a tall horse towards the house.

"What did you do, find the tallest horse you could for me? You did hear me say I was scared, didn't you?" Bobbie asked Scott with a little fear in her voice.

"This here is Tex. He is the offspring of my old horse Patches. He's gentle and a great learner horse. Don't let his size scare you. I've got you. Trust me." Scott replied as he swung his body on top of the horse with ease. He reached down and grabbed Bobbie's hand to help her up. She sat with her chest pressed against his back. "Hold on tight." Scott told her.

The two of them started to ride the fence line while making small talk. Scott explained how he came to live with Lionel.

"I was sent to live here on the rance due to CPS taking me from my father, who was abusive to me and my mother. I love this ranch. We have so many plans. Like I would like to start buying more horses to expand in that area. I'm not sure what is going to happen now."

"I am so sad that my mom refused to talk about my dad." Bobbie told him. "I can't believe she would lie by saying that he didn't want anything to do with her. I guess she just assumed he got the letter. Crazy how life can change due to misunderstandings. I wish she would have reached out and talked to him." Scott agreed.

"I can't imagine what life would have been like if she would have double checked that he did receive that letter. We might have met a lot sooner." Bobbie thought about that for a minute.

"I can't imagine my life any different. I mean, life was good growing up. At least until my mom got sick and I had to work two jobs. Do you know how hard it was to work two jobs just to pay for her medical care?" Scott admitted that he didn't.

"I can't even imagine. I'm so sorry you had to go through that. I bet if I still lived with my dad I would have been in the same situation, but instead of working for his care it would be to pay for his drinking." Bobbie gave him a look that expressed she felt bad for his childhood experience.

"I can't even tell you how hard dating was." Bobbie laughed nervously, trying to change the subject. "I was dating a guy named Bruce before my mom got sick. He was great at first but, when I no longer had time to be with him all the time, he just left. I had been too busy to really care. Like I really did not even miss him. That's sad. Maybe he did me a favor by leaving."

"Sounds like a spoiled jerk to me." Scott said.

By the time they were done with the ride, Tank had the workers meet them at the barn. The ranch had twenty crew members when Scott moved here, but they lost a couple. Fred died when he tried to ride a wild horse while he was drunk. Timmy and James both married and left the ranch. Then they had a couple leave and new ones came, but now they only had about fourteen crew members. When Scott and Bobbie stopped at the barn, Tank helped Bobbie down while Scott walked Tex to his stall. Outside Tank introduced her to the crew.

"This is Mr. James's daughter and that means hands off." Some of the guys were whispering to each other.

"He never mentioned a daughter."

"I wonder why she showed up all of a sudden, when he's sick?" Tank continued to talk over the men.

"If I find anyone even thinking of hitting on her, they will be fired before they can even think of an excuse. Is that clear?"

"Yes Boss." Was echoed back to Tank.

"Good, introduce yourself then get back to work." Each crew member introduced himself and walked back to whatever job they were doing. Tank was the last member and he explained that Scott told him about her and that if she had any questions about the ranch, he would be more than happy to help her. He gave her his phone number in case she needed anything. Scott and Bobbie walked inside to see that Denise had dinner ready on the table.

"Hello, you must be Bobbie. Lionel called and said you would be here. Oh My God! He didn't tell me how much you look like him. Doesn't she look just like him Scott?" Denise was still squeezing Bobbie the whole time she was chatting.

"Um… I think Bobbie is way prettier than Old Man but I can see the resemblance." Scott replied. "Now if you are finished squeezing her, maybe she would like to eat." Denise jumped back and began to apologize for squeezing her.

"We hardly ever get company, so I just get excited." Denise spoke animatedly. As the three of them sat down to dinner they talked about small things. Denise explained to Bobbie how she came to the ranch about the same time as Scott. "Lionel is a great boss. He's fair and he helped me with a lot of legal issues that found me here in Texas. I'm so glad that you got to meet him. He's such a sweet person."

"Wow that was nice of him. So he had you start just because Scott would live here?" Bobbie was trying to piece everything together. Looking at Scott she asked. "Did my father know you before you came to live here?"

"Nope, but he treated me with respect and care from the moment I pulled up, even though I wasn't so respectful." Scott chuckled as he remembered that day so long ago.

After dinner Scott and Bobbie went out on the back porch and just sat quietly; it was a comfortable silence. Bobbie was thinking about all she learned about the man that was her father. Scott was thinking about what Bobbie being here meant for the ranch. He was sure that Lionel was going to leave the ranch to her now. He basically said so when he drew up his will. Scott wasn't mad, he would do the same. He was just worried about what Bobbie would do with it.

"Why did you choose to come to Texas after all?" Scott asked Bobbie, not even looking at her.

"Well you said Lionel was bad off and I have always wanted to meet my father. I figured if I didn't do it now and he didn't make it, that I would always regret not getting on that plane." Bobbie answered.

Again the two of them were quiet for a while, then Bobbie announced that she was going to go to bed and Scott decided he would help her. They left the porch and walked up the stairs. At the bedroom door, Scott had this overwhelming urge to kiss her. He leaned forward and at the last second he kissed her forehead.

"I'm really glad that you chose to come after all." Then Scott turned and went into his room and shut the door. Bobbie stood in the hallway for a moment longer, trying to breathe again. She really thought Scott was going to kiss her and for some reason she wanted him to. Bobbie finally made it into the room and decided to call Lynn back and tell her about her day.

"Hey Lynn, I'm sorry to call you so late. Just wanted to let you know how my day went." Lynn of course was running a mile a minute with a bunch of questions.

"How are you? How is the ranch? Are there any cute cowboys? What did your dad mean when he said that Scott is single but looking at you? Girl, are you going to talk or what?" Bobbie laughed.

"Calm down, breathe. Okay, now the ranch is so gorgeous. I felt right at home the moment my feet hit the ground. Have you ever felt like you were exactly where you were supposed to be? I have never been to Texas or the LJ Ranch, but I know this is where I belong. As for the cowboys, okay, yes there are some cute guys here but I have barely said hello to any of them. Can you believe that the head foreman told all the guys I was off limits, that they couldn't even flirt with me. How embarrassing. As for Scott." Bobbie took a deep breath. "Scott is nice, funny, and sexy as hell. He took me on a horse ride and I was so scared I held on to him the whole time and let me tell you working this ranch has done his body good. I thought I was going to drool right on his back. After dinner he walked me to my room and I thought he was going to kiss me. But he only kissed me on my forehead." Lynn was screaming on the other side of the phone.

"I can't believe you girl! Not even in Texas for a day and you are hooking up with sexy ass cowboys! So how long are you going to stay?" Bobbie didn't have any clue. She didn't make any plans. She just told her bosses what was going on and left Colorado.

"I don't know Lynn, I love it here and I just got here. I plan on getting to know my dad tomorrow and then I'll think about it. I have to go since we'll be up early. I love you and miss you already. Bye." Lynn and Bobbie hung up and Bobbie lay in bed thinking about that almost kiss from Scott until her eyes were too heavy to stay open.

The next morning Scott was already downstairs when Bobbie walked into the kitchen.

"Fifteen minutes then we are heading out to the hospital. Can you be ready or do you need more time?" Scott asked her as she sat in front of a plate of eggs, bacon, biscuits and a glass of orange juice.

"That should be enough time. Thanks." Bobbie quickly ate then went to get ready for a day of sitting in the hospital.

A few minutes later they were walking out to the truck to head to the hospital. They were silent during the drive, both lost in their own thoughts. As they exited the elevator on the seventh floor, Scott stopped to talk to Lionel's nurse. Jealousy shot through Bobbie, even though she knew she had no right to feel that way; she and Scott were not a couple.

"How is my Old Man doing today?" Scott asked the nurse with a smile.

"He's doing great actually. His blood sugar was a little higher than we would like, but all in all he's doing great. He's excited to see you. All night he kept telling us about his daughter he never knew about. I think it was so nice of you to go find her." The nurse told Scott as she ran her fingernail across his forearm. Gently pulling his arm away Scott replied.

"Thank you. I'm sure he would have done the same." He then grabbed Bobbie's hand and pulled her closer to him. "This is Bobbie. She's Lionel's daughter." The nurse introduced herself and made an excuse to leave. Bobbie and Scott walked into Lionel's room. Bobbie noticed that Scott was still holding her hand but said nothing.

"Hey Old Man, I hear you have been nagging these poor nurses." Lionel laughed.

"I'm keeping them occupied. They get bored cleaning bedpans all day. There's my princess. Come over here and give your Old Man a hug." Bobbie walked over to Lionel and leaned down to give him a hug. "How was your night Princess? Did Scotty Boy here show you around the ranch?"

"Yes, he even took me on a ride to check out the fences on the tallest horse I have ever seen."

"I took her out on Tex." Scott chuckled. "Speaking of fences, I need to talk to Joe Murdock and let him know his back fence looks like it could use some mending. But everything else looked good." It got quiet for a little bit since everyone had questions but no one knew where to start.

"So Dad." Bobbie started "How did you and my mom meet?"

"I like this story. Old Man here doesn't talk about his ex-wife very often." Scott said.

CHAPTER 9

"Okay, well kids pull up a chair and let me tell you." Lionel looked off in space for a few seconds trying to think about that time so long ago. "I'm not sure where to start. My parents both died in a car accident when I was nineteen. They were on their way home from a horse show down in San Antonio. It was a fast moving storm. From what I was told, an eighteen wheeler lost control and hit them head on. My parents died immediately. The truck driver was pretty banged up and from what I hear will spend the rest of his life in a wheelchair. I inherited the ranch from my dad. It had been in his family for three generations. I had to drop out of college and learn to ranch. We only had a couple of ranch hands at that time. Tank and Jim, were two of them. Tank was more of a summer hire due to his age. Over the years, I put all my time and energy into that ranch. We grew to twenty ranch hands and I was able to get away for small periods of time. I used to love to get my breakfast at Pop's Diner every morning. One day I was sitting in my usual booth by the front door, and this young woman asked if she could take my order. Like a love sick fool I just stared at her. I couldn't get my mouth to answer. She was the most beautiful angel I had ever seen." Lionel stopped for a second and looked over at his daugher. "You look just like her." Bobbie smiled and blushed at the compliment, then Lionel continued his story. "I must have sat there for a while. She just filled my coffee cup and left. She told Linda, the owner, about me not answering her. Linda told her what my usual was and that's what Allison brought me. I continued to follow her with my eyes the rest of the visit. I didn't have the nerve to even talk to her. So the next day I went back to the Diner hoping she was there again. This time I made myself talk to her. I ordered my usual and when she brought my plate out I introduced myself and asked if she was new since I had never seen her before. She responded that her name was Allison and she was staying with her Aunt Linda for the summer and would be helping out. I didn't have anything else to say, so after I finished eating, I just waved and left the diner. Later that night Tank was telling me how the rodeo was coming the following weekend and asked if I was going. I told Tank to get himself a date that I was going to ask that waitress at Pop's Diner. So the next day when she brought my plate, I asked her to go to the rodeo with me. She, of course, told me no. I mean I was the creepy guy who just stared at her when I would come into the Diner. But when I want something I get it. So later that day I had a bouquet of flowers sent to the Diner with a note that again asked if she would go to the rodeo with me. The next morning I sat at my usual table and when she brought my breakfast I asked if she got my flowers. She smiled the prettiest smile I had ever seen and acknowledged that she did get them. She thanked me, but still refused to go to the rodeo with me. So later that day I had some chocolates sent to the Diner. Every day she said no and every day I sent her something else. First it was flowers, then chocolates, then balloons, then flowers and balloons. That Friday she finally sat down when I was done eating and asked me why I wanted to go with her so badly. I just told her that she was the prettiest thing I had ever seen and just wanted to get to know her. So she finally agreed to go with me. I picked her up at the Diner. She was wearing a short flowing sundress and a pair of cowboy boots. We had a great time and I won her a striped teddy bear at the dart booth." A gasp came from Bobbie at that time. Lionel stopped talking and all eyes turned to her.

"I have a striped teddy bear that was my mother's. I had no idea where she got it, but I remember when she was sad she would hold that bear. No matter how many times we moved, she made sure we had that bear. When she died and I had to get rid of her things, I couldn't get rid of that bear. I still have it. It's actually in my bag at the ranch. I never travel without it." It was silent for a few minutes as each of them thought about what that meant. All those years and she kept a little teddy bear.

"When we get back to the ranch I would love to see that bear." Scott told Bobbie and Lionel continued his story.

"We ate cotton candy and funnel cakes. We rode every ride they had, some twice. I remember the last ride before I had to take her home. We were going to ride the Ferris wheel one more time. I paid the ride attendant ten bucks to stop us at the top. I told him not to move us until she gave me a kiss. We went around once and then the second time he stopped us at the top. She looked out at the city lights and said how beautiful it was. Of course I agreed even though I never took my eyes off Ally. After a few minutes I told her what I had done and that she wouldn't leave until she gave me a kiss. I guess we were taking a little too long because all of a sudden you could hear the ride attendant and a group around him yell out "Kiss him, Kiss him." Ally was so embarrassed that I had done something like that. She did give me a kiss, but it was only a quick peck. I signaled the attendant that I got my kiss. I held her hand all the way back to my truck and once I got her in and buckled I got in and grabbed her hand again. I held it all the way back to the Diner where I was to drop her off. I got out to open the truck door for her and held her hand all the way to the door of the diner. Before she went in I told her what a wonderful time I had and she agreed. I told her that I want to see her again and she said maybe. I surprised her with a kiss. I'm not talking about a kiss on the cheek or a peck on the lips. I mean by the time I let her up she could hardly catch her breath." Again Lionel stopped his story while he silently thought back upon that time. Bobbie had watery eyes just thinking about her parents being happy together and Scott was quiet, just taking in the story. "I couldn't believe that I was the lucky bastard that gave your momma her first kiss." Lionel continued. "The next day I sat in my usual booth waiting to be served when Linda herself came over. She sat in front of me and just stared at me for a little while. I tried to hold my smile while I told her hello, but she kept staring at me. I was getting nervous that she was going to kick me out of the Diner. A while later she tells me that she had not seen Allison smile that big in such a long time. Linda let me know that Allison's daddy had died when she was only a baby; she was about two or three. Then her momma got involved with the wrong crowd and married a man that was violent towards Allison's momma, but never her. Her momma divorced him and married a different man that would bring different women home in front of Allison and her momma. Once her momma divorced him, she moved them to a new state to start fresh, but ended up marrying yet another low life. This one beat on her momma and tried to come into Ally's room. That is why she was at her aunt's. Linda heard about that and sent for Allison herself. She said that she knew I had also had a hard life, with losing both my parents and having to grow up fast and run a ranch. She just wanted to make sure that I wasn't the love them and leave them type of man. I assured her that I only wanted Allison. Shortly after that we were inseparable. She spent a lot of time at the ranch with me and I spent more time in town with her. After about six months of going out, I just knew that I wanted to marry her. She agreed to marry me and we had a small wedding a few months later. I loved my Ally. She was it for me. I have never stopped loving her all these years." Lionel had tears in his eyes as he thought about his Ally dying and him not even knowing.

"Why do you call her Ally? She refused to let anyone call her that." Bobbie asked. She remembered many times when friends of her mother tried to call her Ally. Her mother would tell them, "My name is Allison not Ally." Before Lionel could answer her she understood. Ally was Lionel's name for her.

"So how long were you two married before she left?" Scott asked.

"We were married for seven years, but after five years with no luck having children, Ally came to me and asked how I felt about being foster parents. She said that if we foster children then we can share our love that we have until we have our own family. I agreed since it was something that would make my Ally happy. We were approved to be foster parents but we never heard anything from anyone and I was too busy working the ranch to see how miserable Ally was becoming. We were barely married for seven years when I went into town one morning to get some materials to expand our barn and to make another corral for the horses. It took most of the day and when I got back she was gone. I found a note that said "I'll always love you. Bye, Ally." That was it. I called her Aunt Linda to see if she heard anything but she wasn't talking, just said that she was unhappy and left. That I should just let her go. So I waited by the phone hoping she would call and change her mind. A month later, I did get a call, but not from Ally. It was from Child Protective Services asking if my Scotty here could stay with me. At first I turned them down since Ally wasn't there and I explained that my wife left me and I had no experience with children. Then when they explained that a child was brutally beaten by his own father I just knew that I had to take him in. Not a day goes by that I'm not thankful for taking you in Scott. You have been a great help and I have grown to love you as my own son. I want you to know that." Scott shook his head with tears in his eyes.

"I love you too Old Man. I'm very thankful that you took me in. I would hate to think about what my life would be like had you turned me away." By now Bobbie had tears falling so fast from her eyes that she could no longer stop them. Lionel looked at his newly discovered daughter.

"Bobbie Jean, I do however regret not going after your mother. She was and is the love of my life. Maybe if I had gone after her I would have been in your life. I'm so lucky to get to know you now. I love you with all that I am. I'm so happy that Scott went to find you. I would never have let your mother leave had I known she was pregnant." Bobbie stood up, walked over to Lionel's bed and gave him a hug.

"I love you too, Daddy." The room was quiet for a while as they let everything they just heard sink in. Bobbie was glad to hear that her parents were happy at one time. She could understand how her mother would choose to leave her father instead of having him choose her or the ranch. Scott was sitting quietly thinking about all the years he has loved Lionel as his own father yet he never really told him how he felt. So he turned to Lionel and told him then.

"Old Man, I must say that we aren't usually so sappy, but I have to tell you that I love you. I love that you took me in and showed me that violence is not the answer. You have shown me more love and understanding than my own parents. I remember my mom used to go into another room while my dad would beat on me. Instead of standing up to him and protecting me as a parent should, she allowed the beatings to happen to me. I may not have told you all these years how thankful I am for you. I love you like you were my own father. Truth be told, that's what I have been telling people for the last couple of years. I know that we haven't told each other, but I'm not going to let a day go by that I don't tell you how much I love you. I love you Old Man." Scott walked over to Lionel's bed and gave him a tight hug. "Okay, now that I've cried like a girl, I need to go check on some things and make that phone call to Joe Murdock about his fence. I'll be in the lobby if you need me." Scott walked out. It again got quiet as what Scott just admitted sank in. Neither Bobbie nor Lionel could imagine living his life.

"I may have been raised by a single parent, but she was always there for me. I may be upset with her for not allowing you into my life, but she would never hurt me like that or allow anyone else to hurt me." Bobbie quietly told Lionel.

CHAPTER 10

"So Princess, tell me about you and what all I missed." Lionel requested of Bobbie.

"Well this is hard since I hate to talk about myself and I'm not sure what to say. Let's see, I'm twenty two and I'm single. My last boyfriend, Bruce, left me when I had to take care of mom. We were together for almost a year and I have to say, I didn't even miss him when he left. I'm not sure if it's because I was so busy with mom or I just could care less. Anyway, that was about four years ago. I have dated a few times since then, but just never found any-one worth my time. I work two jobs. I'm a waitress during the day and then I work at the local bowling alley at night. If I keep up the hours I have now, I'll have moms medical bills paid off in about two years. Then I'm thinking of trying to save some money and move into a bigger apartment." Lionel stopped her from talking by asking her a question.

"Are you still paying your mother's medical bills four years after her death?"

"Yeah, it's not a big deal, I'm almost done." They are both quiet and then Bobbie started her story again. "Let's see... I was born in Denver, Colorado, but we moved all around the state when I was younger. It was not until my preteens that I begged mom to stay in one place so I could make a real friend. So we moved to

Boulder and have been there ever since. I met my best friend, Lynn Daniels, when I started the fifth grade. We have been close ever since, she's the one you were talking to on the phone yesterday. I had just started to go to college when mom got sick. I knew she needed me, so I pushed college off and just helped her. With the bills and everything, I had to sell our house and we moved into a small two bedroom apartment, which is where I live now." Lionel just sat there and waited for her to continue, but she never started talking again.

"How do you like Texas so far?" Bobbie looked at Lionel like he was crazy. She just told him how hard she had it and he was asking about how she liked Texas.

"So far it's great from what I have seen. However, I have only been to the airport, the hospital, and the ranch. But it's all nice. I feel a sense of belonging here. Does that make sense?" Just then Scott came into the room.

"Sorry to bother you. I need to head back to the ranch and I'm not sure if I'll be able to come back before visiting hours are over. Would it be okay if I went ahead and took you home now? I could try to get a ranch hand to come get you later, but we have a small problem at the ranch." Bobbie agreed to go back with him. They both gave Lionel a hug and told him they would be back first thing in the morning.

Lionel sat on his bed for a little while, just thinking about his daughter. He still couldn't believe he had a daughter. She seemed like a smart girl. Lionel fell asleep for a while. When he woke up he decided to call his lawyer.

"Kyle this is Lionel. I need to speak to you as soon as possible. I need to make changes to my will. I'm currently in the hospital and it's not looking good. The sooner we take care of this the better." Lionel hung up the phone hoping that Kyle Bradshaw would check his messages soon and get back to him. He planned to have Scott and Bobbie share the ranch; they would each get half. The same stipulations would apply where they would need to keep as many of the ranch hands as possible. He had seen that look on Scott's face all day as he tried to secretly watch Bobbie.

Bobbie didn't do such a great job of hiding her attraction either. He knew Scott would make a great husband to any woman. It was time for him to settle down. Bobbie seemed to be dependable and trustworthy. Who continues to pay medical bills when it's not their responsibility? He made a mental note to have Scott pay off the remaining bills tomorrow. He also needed to find out what Bobbie's plans were. As he was thinking about his kids, his doctor knocked and came in.

"Mr. James, I have the results from your last test. Things don't look too good. I'm afraid it seems your cancer has spread and we're not able to do anything more for you. I'm sorry. We could give you morphine in the IV or we can send you home with our hospice care." The doctor stood there quietly, allowing Lionel to digest this information.

"How long are we talking Doc?"

"It's hard to say Mr. James." The doctor said sadly. "My guess is no longer than a month; that is if no other complications pop up. That's just a guess, but to be honest I'm not sure you have that long. Are your affairs in order?"

"Wow! Wow! I don't know what to say. I have contacted my lawyer and set up my will, but I just called to make some changes. I'm hoping to hear from him soon. As for staying here or going home, let me think on that for a day or two. I really didn't know it was this bad." Lionel told the doctor as he choked up on the last few words.

"No problem, just let me know. In the meantime, if there's anything I can do for you please let me know."

After the doctor left, Lionel took his pillow and covered his face as he silently cried. He never cried, but tonight he did. He cried for Scott, who still had a lot to learn. He loved Scott as his own son. Then there was Bobbie Jean. The biological daughter he just met. He wanted to know her. He wanted her to know him and know that he already loved her more than anything. He cried for all the years he could have had with his Ally. Life just didn't seem fair sometimes. He cried himself to sleep.

CHAPTER 11

"Sorry about pulling you away, but we need to help Mr. Murdock with his fence." Scott told Bobbie as he drove them back to the ranch. "Some of his cattle are getting out and his neighbor on the other side is trying to steal them."

"I'd like to watch if I won't be in the way." Bobbie said.

"Of course you can come. I just need you to promise to listen to me out there so nothing dangerous happens to you."

"Promise." She agreed with a smile.

After they got the cattle back on the J&R Ranch and fixed the fence, both Bobbie and Scott were exhausted.

"Is that something you have to do all the time?" Bobbie asked.

"Not so much as an emergency like we did tonight. Usually if our fences are broken and our animals get loose we just gather them up, send them back and fix the fence. However, his neighbor isn't as friendly and believes if they come to his yard he should have the right to keep them. So we had to hurry and gather his cattle and fix his fence. It's happened a time or two. That is why I usually take a ride along the fence line once or twice a week. Thank you by the way." Scott loved how Bobbie was willing to help when needed, but stayed back when told to. She was also the one to find the baby calf under the tree in the lower valley. By the time Scott and Bobbie made it back to the ranch, Denise had their dinner ready.

"This looks delicious Denise. Thank you. I'm not sure I can eat all this. I'm so tired." Bobbie said. As they ate quietly, she thought about how much fun she had. She had never really seen a bunch of guys come together to help each other out. She wished she had this kind of life growing up. "Well, I'm tired so I'm going to call it an early night. See you tomorrow Denise and thanks again for dinner. Scott, what time should I be ready tomorrow?" Bobbie asked as she walked her plate to the sink.

"Oh, um, visiting hours don't start until eight tomorrow so I say get a little sleep and be ready at about seven thirty." Scott replied. As they were walking to their room Scott stopped Bobbie in the hall. "Um… I was wondering if you would like to go to Pop's Diner with me tomorrow for breakfast." Scott asked.

"Okay, that sounds great." Bobbie smiled a flirty innocent smile. Scott again leaned down to give her a kiss, but at the last moment just gave her one on the cheek. They went to their separate rooms and fell asleep.

The next morning Bobbie woke up to her cell phone ringing.

"Hey, Lynn. What are you doing up so early?" Lynn didn't answer, she just launched in with her own questions.

"So did you have a good day yesterday? You never called me back."

"Yeah." She answered with a smile. "I had a great day. I got to spend a few hours with my dad. We talked about how my parents met. We talked about my mom and can you believe after all these years he's still in love with her?"

"Shut up. I mean that's over twenty years. He still loved her? I mean I loved your mom too, but to love her for twenty years with no contact."

"Crazy, I know." She laughed. "Oh guess where I'm going this morning?"

"Girl where are you going? You better not be holding out on me."

"Scott asked me to go to the diner with him. I'm not sure if it's just because it's on the way or if it's something more.

"I bet he wants this to be a date. You should ask him, or I can if you want me to." Lynn offered.

"NO! I'll just play it by ear for now, besides I think he was going to kiss me again. I'm not sure; maybe it's just me wanting him to kiss me.

"You should have kissed him then."

"Someone is knocking on my door, I have to go. Talk to you later. Love you. Bye." Bobbie hung up and called for them to come in.

"I was checking to see if you were ready to go? I already told Denise not to cook for us; that we'll be going to the Diner and probably be out past lunch." Scott said.

"Yeah let's go. I'm so excited to see my dad again. Is it weird that I feel like I have known him my whole life? I wish that we had been a part of each other's lives this whole time." Scott pulled Bobbie into a hug.

"I know that's exactly how he feels too. We talk at night over the phone. We have always talked at night before bed. Since the day I moved in with him at the age of ten, we have never not talked at night. We talked about you and how much he already loves you. He regrets letting your mother leave. You have to know that if he had any idea that she was pregnant, he wouldn't have let her go."

"Yes, I do believe that." Bobbie wiped a tear from her face. "I guess there's no reason to wish for what could have been; I need to worry more about what is. Let's go, I'm hungry. Plus I want to see this diner that my parents met at." Scott held Bobbie's hand all the way to the truck. He opened her door for her and made sure she buckled before he shut her door and made his way to his side of the truck.

At the Diner, he showed her the table where Lionel met her mother. "This is your dad's booth." Scott explained. "Whenever he comes in here, this is where he sits. He will literally wait for someone to leave instead of taking a different seat.

They both ordered a coffee and the daily special. As they were sitting there waiting for their order a woman with stringy black hair walked up to the table.

"Hey Scott. Are you ready for that second date yet?" Scott gave Bobbie an annoyed look.

"Bethany I've told you there will be no second date. I've asked you to please leave me alone. Don't make me look like a jerk in front of my date." That was when Bethany looked over to Bobbie.

"Why can you date her and not me?" Scott ignored her at first, but she was trying to make a scene. Scott looked to Bobbie and whispered.

"I'm so sorry about this." Then he turned his attention to Bethany. "Bethany, you are a drugged out beauty queen who lost her looks years ago. You're a thief who tried to steal my wallet on our date. You didn't even try to hide it. You're trying to date me because you think I have money. I have asked you to stay away from me. I don't like people like you. Now leave." Bethany just looked at Bobbie, then at Scott, and then back at Bobbie.

"Yeah well, he's not that good in bed anyway." She sneered before stalking out of the diner.

"She wouldn't know since I never slept with her." Bobbie just laughed.

"I've had my share of exes also, I understand." Scott laughed.

"What do you know about exes?" He was seriously curious.

"Well, I had my first boyfriend in seventh grade, but he only lasted about a week. When I wouldn't let him feel me up, he decided I wasn't worth his time. Then I dated a guy from seventh grade to eighth grade, but we were more friends than boyfriend and girlfriend; we are still good friends. I was single for a little while, then in tenth grade, I dated the star basketball player and we were good until he went off to college. I knew what would happen, so we decided to break up then instead of when he cheated on me with college girls. Again, I'm still good friends with him also. Then there were a couple of guys my Junior and Senior year, but nothing serious until Bruce, and like I said his leaving was hardly noticed. Anyway." She shrugged and changed the subject. "Tell me more about what it was like growing up with my dad." They talked about everything from school to childhood memories.

"I remember this one time I had a school play. It was like early on when I was placed at the ranch. I was on stage and I forgot my lines. Lionel had worked with me every night. I was standing there looking out at the crowd who was just staring at me. I thought I was going to pee myself. All of a sudden from this quiet auditorium, Lionel starts to call out my lines. I picked them up pretty quick after that but I will always remember him standing up for me." Scott told her.

"Wow. Sounds like he was a great father."

"He was." Scott said. "I wish that you could have had the opportunity to experience that."

"Me too." Bobbie closed her eyes and took a deep calming breath. Scott reached across the table and took her hand. She squeezed his hand and tried to smile. "So what were your biological parents like?" She asked because one, she needed to change the subject; she didn't want to think about all she'd missed out on. And two, because she really wanted to get to know Scott better.

"They weren't good people." Scott shook his head. "My father used to beat me, badly. I ended up in the hospital several times. My mom just let it happen. It was a living hell. I have tried over the years to find some good quality, but I can't."

"Oh Scott." Bobbie's eyes widened and squeezed his hand again. "That's terrible." Scott just shrugged.

"You'd be surprised what you get used to." He huffed out a breath. "Anyway when I was ten, CPS placed me with Old Man. He made sure I was never hurt again. He showed me what a father was supposed to be like." Bobbie gave a weird look.

"Why do you always call him Old Man?"

"Oh, I guess it is just a term of endearment now. When I first came he was all nice and trying to be helpful. I called him an Old Man to make him man but he only laughed. I just kept calling him

Old Man even when he told me to call him Lionel. Now I do it out of love. I don't know calling him Lionel just doesn't feel right."

"I'm so glad he was there for you." Bobbie said.

"He really was. Especially when they tried to make me go back to my parents."

"They tried to give you back?" Bobbie was outraged.

"Yeah, when I was seventeen, but Old Man put up a fight and I was able to stay with him."

"Thank God." She said with relief.

"I had to go stay with them every other weekend for a while, but my father couldn't stay sober so that didn't last long. One weekend he hit me."

"No." Bobbie gasped. "What did you do?"

"Well I wasn't a weak little kid anymore. Seven years of working the ranch made me a whole lot tougher. I wanted to fight him back, but then I thought about how your dad taught me never to fight unless you have to. So I just pushed him off of me and went home. Lionel called the cops the second he saw the bruise on my cheek and he got arrested for child abuse."

"What about your mom?"

"She did nothing, same as always." He shook his head. "With that being said, my mom contacted me recently. My parents finally got divorced and now my mom is trying to be a part of my life, but I'm not ready for that. I understand that she's still my mom, but where was she when I needed her. Now that she's sober and getting her life on track, she wants to be a part of my life. I just don't think I owe her anything just because she gave birth to me. Old Man keeps telling me I should at least hear her out and start allowing her in my life. I'm just not ready. Do you think that makes me a bad guy?" Scott truly wanted to know how she felt about this. Actually he really wanted to know how she felt about him. The more they talked, the more he liked her. He had to admit that when he met her in Colorado, he wasn't too happy with her. When she did come to Texas, he was thinking she was only after her dad's money. However, the more he got to know her, the more he liked her. He couldn't believe that he almost kissed her again last night. She must think he was a pervert.

"Well, she's your mom, but like you said, she never acted the part. She should have defended you when you were being beaten up by your dad. I can't believe she would walk away and allow it to happen." Bobbie shook her head. " But I guess I can also see that if she has changed, she might want to make amends and try to have some sort of relationship with you. Look at me and my dad. Circumstances might be different, but I'm twenty two and I just found him. I know he's sick and I'm trying to make any kind of relationship with him that I can. Life is too short sometimes. So no, it doesn't make you a bad guy. I'll say that if she did leave your dad and has changed her life, you might want to start slow. Maybe meet at the Diner for coffee the first time. Hear what she has to say and then from there you can decide if you want to have a relationship. I would make sure you ask all the questions you have, regardless of how sad she gets. She owes you that much." Bobbie stopped talking and took a drink of her coffee.

Scott just stared at her with awe. How could someone he barely knows just get him? He always thought he was a complex guy with all his life's baggage, but she got him.

"That's some good advice and I'll definitely take you up on that. Maybe next week I'll call and set up a coffee date with her. That way I can get my answers then leave and think about them before I decide if I want a relationship. Thanks." It was Scott's turn to change the subject. "So, how do you like the ranch? You did an awesome job with the fence fixing last night." Bobbie blushed at the compliment. She was so bad with compliments; Lynn always made fun of her for it.

"The ranch is so beautiful and peaceful. I feel so at home there. I always loved Colorado, but the moment my feet hit the ground on the ranch I just felt like I came home. That is crazy and so cliché, I know. I hope to be able to learn to ride a horse on my own before I have to leave. Maybe you can help me with that?" Bobbie asked. Scott got a huge smile on his face. Maybe she did feel about him as he did her.

"Yeah, sounds good. Dreamsicle is a great horse to learn on." They finished their breakfast and headed to the hospital. Scott took Bobbie's hand as they exited the truck. Walking hand in hand was nice. Neither one discussed their feelings for one another. As they exited the elevator on Lionel's floor, Scott again stopped and talked to the nurse on duty.

"How is my Old Man today?" This time the nurse was not as smiling as yesterday. Bobbie wondered if maybe that was because Scott was holding her hand.

"Actually he's doing better than last night. We had some issues. I'll get the doctor to come talk to you. Give me just a few minutes to document his chart. You can wait in that room." She said as she pointed to the room behind the nurse's station. The nurse quickly wrote all the information she needed into his chart and left to find the doctor.

Shortly after the doctor came in, followed by the nurse. He shook each of their hands.

"Well, I'll explain to you what I told Mr. James. I'm sorry to have to tell you this, but we found that the cancer is spreading. We can help with the pain, but the truth is he doesn't have a lot of time left. I'm sorry." They discussed his prognosis for a few minutes then the doctor and nurse turned and walked out of the room. Scott pulled Bobbie into a hug.

"Okay, we need to go in there and pretend we don't know. We have to put on a brave face. Can you do that?" Bobbie wiped a tear from her cheek.

"Yeah, I can." They both took a deep breath and walked into Lionel's room. "Hey Daddy, how are you feeling this morning?" Bobbie asked as she leaned over to give her dad a hug.

"Better now that my princess is here. How was your morning?" Scott decided to join in the conversation.

"I took her to the Diner and sat at your booth. Is the booth you sit at now the same as when you met Allison?"

Smiling at them, Lionel answered that yes, that was the same booth. They talked about the Diner and how Linda passed away a while ago. The Diner was left to a waitress who had worked there since Linda opened the doors. They had kept everything the same, from the menu to the booths.

"Sorry we had to leave so soon yesterday." Scott told Lionel. "The cattle got loose from Joe's ranch and ended up on the wrong neighbor's ranch. And you know how Old Man Henderson gets about loose cattle. But, I would have you know, that Bobbie here was a big help. She found the baby calf that we couldn't find and she helped with the fence. You would have been proud." Bobbie of course was blushing like a fool at hearing people talk about her.

"I'm not surprised, she does have James blood after all. Speaking of James blood, I need to talk to you both." Lionel asked them both to pull up a chair closer to him so he did not have to yell across the room. "This is hard, but I need to say it. I talked to the doctor last night and he doesn't think I have much longer." At these words all three of them had watery eyes. Bobbie gasped as tears rolled down her face. "I called my lawyer and I'm waiting on him to call me back. I plan on making changes to my will." Lionel looked right at Scott. "Scott, you know I love you as my own. Never doubt that son. You hear me?" Scott wasn't really able to talk so he nodded his head in agreement. "At the time I made my will, I didn't know about my princess over here. Bobbie Jean, I know we just met, but I love you. I love you as if I have known you all your life. I hate that we don't have much time together, but know I love you. I had Scott pay off the rest of your mother's medical bills, as well as your credit cards. Please don't get mad, this was my idea. Your mother's medical bills should have been my responsibility. I loved her, dammit, I still love her. I want you to be able to do what you want and not be held back by financial responsibilities that were never yours. So anyway, I want to change my will. Instead of Scott inheriting the ranch, I want to split it in half. Scott will only be inheriting half and the other half will go to Bobbie. However, I still have my stipulations. You must try to keep as many of the current workers as you can. Now I'll add you can't sell your half of the ranch to anyone but each other. I also stipulate that this ranch be a partnership and not cut down the middle and have two ranches.

Am I making myself clear?" Bobbie was sobbing loudly now and Scott pulled her into his arms.

"I get you Old Man and I agree with the stipulations. When is Mr. Bradshaw going to draw these up?"

"I have called him numerous times with no answer. I believe he's on that cruise with his wife. If I'm not mistaken, he should return tomorrow night. So let's say Wednesday be ready to sign. Is all of this alright with you Princess?" Bobbie, who was still silently sobbing in Scott's arms, shook her head in acknowledgment.

"I'm so sorry. I hate this. I just found you and now I might lose you. I love you Daddy. I don't want to lose you. I wish there was something I could do." Lionel reached out for his daughter.

"Come here Princess. Always know that I loved you. No matter if I only knew about you for a couple of days. I love you. I know this is sad, but last night when the doctor told me, I was thinking that I can rest easy knowing that you're taken care of now. No more struggling, no more thinking about your next meal. I'll also be able to fix my one regret. When the good Lord takes me, the first thing I'm going to do is go find your momma and give her a kiss she will never forget. I'll be with her again, my beautiful daughter. Now let's talk about you. How is that friend of yours, Lynn? I think she needs to come for a visit. I talked to a couple of nurses here and I asked around. You can tell her that the nurses seem to think my ranch is full of sexy cowboys." Bobbie burst out laughing as well as Scott and Lionel.

That broke the ice and then they started to talk about Lynn and how she was outgoing and beautiful. A while later, Bobbie called Lynn and Lionel got on the phone. He told Lynn what each nurse said about his ranch hands.

"I think you would like Randy. he's about your age. The nurses say he's a good guy and that he's not a player, but that he isn't innocent either." Lionel laughed into the phone, listening to Lynn. "Scott? No, I don't think Scott is available. He might be single, but I think he has his eyes on my princess." Lionel looked at Scott with humor on his face. "Yes, of course he's a good guy.

I would never let anyone near my daughter if I didn't think they were good enough. Okay Lynn, my lunch is coming down the hall, I have to go, but I look forward to seeing you soon. Okay bye." Lionel hung up the phone and handed it back to Bobbie. "I like her. She really seems to care about you. She's going to be visiting us soon. I think I'll have Randy show her around. What do the two of you think? Do you think Randy and her would hit it off?" Lionel was excited. Just then a nurse entered his room with his lunch.

"Old Man, while you eat your lunch I'm going to take Bobbie down to the cafeteria to get us something and be right back. Until then you might want to think about watching what you say when certain people are here. I can't believe you would just talk about me liking Bobbie right in front of her." Scott walked out with Lionel laughing. He grabbed Bobbie's hand and walked her down to the cafeteria. They both picked out a cheeseburger and fries and found an empty table in the corner.

"I can't believe how you and my dad paid off all my bills without you telling me. Why?" She asked and Scott set his burger back on the plate.

"Lionel wanted that to be a surprise. We have software that runs a background check for when we hire new people. I ran your name and address and saw your credit report. I just paid off anything that was on there. If there's anything not paid let me know and I'll pay it off as well. I hope you're not mad. That's just who your dad is. Did you know he paid for a house to be built for Tank's mom a few years ago? There was a bad storm and her roof collapsed. He had a brand new house built and made it handicapped accessible for her as well. The thing was that Tank never told your dad about the house. Tank went to the bank to apply for a loan to have it fixed. The bank called to verify employment and your dad talked to the loan officer and explained that he does work for him and to gently refuse the loan. Tank was hurt at first because your dad went behind his back, but he knew he would never have been able to give her that kind of house. He has helped with hospital bills for many of the ranch hand's family members. He's just a giving person. He has never once asked for anything in return. So please don't be mad." Bobbie had tears in her eyes thinking about what a wonderful man her dad was.

"I'm not mad, I was just blindsided I guess. I love to hear stories about him. What was he like when you were younger? I would always daydream about him coming to look for me. I can't imagine him knowing and not doing anything about it. I wonder what my mom thought all these years. He doesn't seem to be the kind of man to ignore his family and my mom must have known that about him. I wonder now why she did not try harder to let him know about me." Scott pulled Bobbie into his arms again and let her cry. He had wondered that same question since he found that letter. "Oh my god, I'm so sorry, I have never cried so much in my life. It's just all so much. I mean I went from not knowing my dad's name to finding him and loving him to losing him all within a few days. I'm usually a lot tougher." Bobbie stated.

"I would be just as emotional." Scott reassured her. "Seeing Lionel in the hospital and knowing he doesn't have long is hard to hear." He just held her until she stopped crying.

Once they gathered their emotions, they headed back to his room. He was sleeping so they just sat and quietly talked about the ranch. Scott told stories about each crew member and why they have some of their rules in place. He explained that Lionel wanted no drama to come between his employees so he made a rule that the ranch hands couldn't date Denise.

"Is that why Tank made a big announcement about me being off limits?" Bobbie asked.

"That was part of it, the other part is he can see how I look at you and didn't want me to fight anyone." Scott admits. "Although if you ask me, I think Denise and Tank have been together for a while now. I can't prove it, but I have my suspicions. I also think Old Man knows about them but chooses not to say anything."

"Damn right I know boy. I knew since the first time she snuck down to his cottage a few years ago. It took them both many years to show each other how they felt. She thought she was all sneaky waiting until I was in bed. Tank is a big guy with a deep voice. Noises carry in the night. That's all I'm saying." All three burst into a fit of laughter.

"Oh My Gosh, you heard them. That's embarrassing." Bobbie commented.

"Actually, I recently talked to Tank about his relationship with Denise. Tank has had his eyes on her since she got here but he knew she wasn't ready. So the first few years they were just friends. For a few years after that Tank would flirt with her but it was never reciprocated. Then a few more years of them flirting back and forth until they started to secretly meet up. I think he's going to propose soon. Tank doesn't want to leave the ranch and hopes to buy an acre or two in the far west corner so he can still be close. He has actually started to build a small house for the two of them. I have it ready as a wedding present to give them the two acres. Well I guess you two can see to it that it happens. I may not be around." No one spoke for a few minutes as it hit them how close his time was coming. Scott excused himself from the room to make a phone call.

"Tank, hey it's Scott. I need to ask you something and I want you to be honest."

"Boy when have I ever not been honest with you?" Tank answered.

"I talked to Old Man and he said you were planning on proposing to Denise."

"Damn him. He could never keep a secret. Yes. I'm planning to ask her. Why?" Ignoring his question Scott continued.

"Do you have a ring already?"

"What kind of man proposes without a ring? Again Why?"

"Great, do you already have a plan to propose?"

"Well not quite, I was planning to wait until it felt right, you know? Now for the last time, will you tell me why you're all of a sudden so interested in my life?"

"You don't?" Scott asked, ignoring yet again Tank's questions. "That's even better, listen. The doctor said that Old Man doesn't have long. I know that he would love to see you two married, but we won't have that long. I was thinking, if you could get Denise to the hospital, you could propose in front of him. That would make him happy. What do you say?"

"I'm not sure. I mean the hospital isn't very romantic. She deserves romance. She deserves to have this big display. I just don't think that is the right option for me."

"Great, this is going to mean so much to the Old Man. See you within the hour."

"WHAT? Did you not hear me? I said No. Sorry Scott, I can't do it like that." Scott just laughed

"No worries, I'll take care of everything. You just bring the ring and your girl. Bye." Scott hung up the phone before Tank could say anything else. He walked back into Lionel's room and waited a few minutes then asked to speak to Bobbie outside. "Okay, look, I know how much seeing Tank and Denise marry would mean to your father. I also know that is unlikely to happen. So I called Tank and he agreed to propose to Denise in front of Old Man today. I told him I would get some flowers for him to give to Denise, so could you go to the gift shop with me to help pick them out?"

"That's so awesome Scott; yes I'll help however I can. I'm so excited. Let's go."

Scott grabbed Bobbie's hand and they walked to the gift shop and purchased a couple bouquets of roses and balloons.

"I may or may not have tricked Tank. He didn't actually say he would propose. I just didn't take no for an answer and then hung up on him. So he might be a little mad when he gets here. If he gets here." Bobbie hit him on his chest with the back of her hand.

"Scott, are you crazy? That's so messed up. You better hope they show up." They walked back to the seventh floor and left the items with the nursing staff so that Lionel wouldn't see them. They went back into Lionel's room and made idle chit chat about nothing important. Bobbie told Lionel that she wanted to learn to ride a horse and that Scott agreed to train her. Scott talked about ideas he had for the ranch; they still needed to finish the kitchen upgrade.

"Are you talking about my kitchen again Scott Wilson?" Denise walked into the room. Bobbie and Scott stood to welcome Denise and Tank with hugs. Then Denise and Tank bent over to hug Lionel. They all sat down and talked about what was happening at the ranch. Scott gave Tank a look that said "go ahead." Tank gave him a look that said "NO"; this went on for a bit. Everyone in the room stopped talking and it was getting kind of uncomfortable.

"Um… Lionel." Tank cleared his throat. He wasn't nervous on the phone with Scott but now that it was time, he was really nervous. "You and I have talked about this before. I think it is time." Tank looked at Denise with a "forgive me" look as he rubbed the back of his neck. Denise's eyes got huge when she figured out what they were talking about. The first rule Mr. James told her was that the ranch hands were off limits. Tank continued. "Everyone knows I have been seeing Denise for quite some time. Since we were so unsuccessful at hiding it. I know that rules were hands off the cook. I'm sorry; I can't hide it anymore. I feel that she deserves the respect of not hiding our relationship anymore. With that being said…" Tank pulled the ring from his pocket and went down on one knee in front of Denise. "Denise. My love. I have loved you since the day you came to the ranch. I tried to fight my feelings for you but they are just too strong. I hate that we had to hide our relationship from everyone. I want everyone to know that you're mine and I'm yours. Denise, please! Say that you will wear this ring and become my wife." Denise had tears rolling down her face, as did Bobbie. The guys in the room all had watery eyes.

"Yes, yes Tank I'll marry you. I love you." A few nurses brought in the flowers and balloons Scott was holding behind the nurses station and everyone congratulated the newly engaged couple. Lionel wiped tears from his eyes and hugged Denise.

"I'm so happy for you two." He looked at Tank. "It's about time. I was beginning to think you were going to chicken out. I was going to set her up with someone else already." Lionel joked and Tank gave him a hard look with a grunt.

Once everything calmed down, Lionel was all smiles but fell asleep. Tank and Denise made their way out the door. Scott called after Denise to tell her to take the night off, that he and Bobbie would cook for themselves.

Bobbie watched her father sleep. She had noticed that he seemed to be losing energy so much faster the more she saw him. The first day she was here, he stayed awake all day, but each day that passed, he seems to be sleeping more and more. She decided to pull Scott into the hall and ask if he'd noticed anything as well.

"Scott, have you noticed how much less energy he has each day? He has slept most of today and he's sleeping again." Scott agreed that he did seem to be getting weaker.

"Let's go ahead and head home so he can get some rest. Mr. Bradshaw should be here tomorrow night. That will help his stress level. Let's go say goodnight." Scott walked Bobbie back into Lionel's room.

"Daddy, we have to go. Go ahead and get your rest. We will be back tomorrow to see you. I love you." Bobbie leaned over and gave her dad a hug. Scott also told him he loved him and gave him a hug. They walked to the nurses station and left their names and numbers in case anything happened.

The two held hands and walked out of the hospital. They went back to the Diner for dinner and each had a cheeseburger with fries and a milkshake. They sat and talked about everything that had happened that day. They were excited about the engagement of Tank and Denise.

"So have you ever thought about getting married?" Scott asked Bobbie.

"Truthfully, every little girl can imagine her wedding. However, as you grow up and life gets more real you start to lose that dream. It's been many years since I thought about marriage for myself. With mom getting sick and then having to repay her bills, I didn't even have time to date, much less be in a relationship where it could lead to marriage. But I would love to get married one day and have children. What about you? Have you thought about getting married?"

"To be honest I didn't have that urge for a long time. I still have some demons to fight from my childhood. The thought of children used to scare me. I thought I would be like my dad. One night during our nightly talks, Old Man and I talked about my fears. He said, "Damn right you are like your Old Man. I think I raised you right, so you shouldn't be worried about being like your biological dad since I'm nothing like him." That night I started to think about settling down. I'm thirty two and not getting any younger. Being ready and finding someone are two different things. There was no one I wanted to even try to get to know until you came to town." Scott stopped talking to give Bobbie time to understand what he was saying. Bobbie's head snapped up to face him. "Let's play a game, have you ever played would you rather?" Bobbie laughed and shook her head yes.

"Would you rather be rich or smart?" Scott started first and his questions were easy enough. Bobbie thought about it for a minute.

"Smart because I could learn to be rich."

"Would you rather be with a gold digger or a prostitute?"

"What? What kind of question is that? I would be with a prostitute; at least that way the money would be coming in instead of out."

"Would you rather fight an elephant or a moose?"

"Aw, do I have to fight one. I would love to snuggle up with a Moose. I guess I would fight the elephant." After a few rounds of crazy questions Scott used his next questions to find out more about her.

"Would you rather have a church wedding or a backyard wedding?"

"When I was younger I always dreamed of a big church wedding. Me, walking down the aisle in my long white dress. But now, I think I would prefer a ranch wedding." She started to giggle with this.

"Would you rather marry in Texas or Colorado?"

"Again, same as before. I would see myself in Colorado, but since being here in Texas, I would love to marry in Texas."

"Would you rather have a big wedding or a small wedding?"

"A midsize wedding. Is that an answer?" Then he decided to change tactics so she didn't catch on.

"Would you rather be a doctor or a lawyer?"

"I would rather be a doctor. But don't tell Peter, my best friend's dad."

"Would you rather live in the city or the country?"

"I'm a city girl who happens to love the country. If I had to pick one it would country, close to the city"

"Would you rather drive a truck or a car?"

"I have always liked trucks."

"Would you rather live on land or water?"

"I would live on land next to the water." Bobbie answered. Penelope walked by asking if there was anything else they needed before she closed up. Scott didn't even notice the time.

"Sorry Penelope, we'll head out now. Here let me carry these dishes to the back for you and help you clean." Scott offered.

"No you two go on and have some fun. I was just checking on yall." They said their goodbyes to Penelope and left the diner. But Scott didn't want the date to end.

"Hey, would you like to check out Buckaroo's, it's a dance hall. My friend Billy and his band should be playing tonight." Bobbie got excited.

"I would love to. I haven't been dancing in a long time." Scott got a smile on his face as he walked her to his truck and opened her door.

Once inside the dance hall, Bobbie's body started to move with the music causing Scott to laugh to himself.

"Do you want to head to the dance floor or do you want to go grab a table before they all get taken?" Bobbie looked around and suggested they get a table.

"It looks like they fill up fast. We should grab a table while we can. Besides I could probably use a drink before I get out there in front of all these strangers." Scott asked her more questions about herself.

"So do you go dancing a lot back in Colorado?"

"Lynn drags me out sometimes. I usually put up a fight, but she wins. If you ever meet her you'll see." After some time drinking and talking Scott finally got her on the dance floor. They danced to almost every song. They would start to head back to the table when she would pull him back on the dance floor. "Oh I love this song." It was a few hours later when Billy came on to say that this was the last set. The bartender then called out.

"Last call." Bobbie looked at the clock.

"Oh my goodness! Look at the time, it's after two in the morning. I can't believe we have stayed out so late. We should get going so we can visit Dad tomorrow." They got up and were heading to the truck when Scott stopped. He had the worst feeling wash over him. He couldn't explain it, but he knew something was wrong.

"Bobbie, we have to go back to the hospital right now. I just know something is wrong. Do you want me to drop you off to get some sleep or do you want to ride with me? It could be nothing, but I just have this feeling."

"Me too." Bobbie squeezed his hand. "Let's go." They ran to the truck and raced to the hospital.

At this hour of morning no one was on the streets. They made it to the hospital in record time and both raced into the elevator and pressed the seventh floor. Just as the doors opened, they heard an alarm for code blue. They started towards Lionel's room when a male nurse stopped them and told them to wait in the waiting room. An hour and a half later the doctor walked out and told them they tried to do everything they could, but Lionel didn't make it.

"NO!!!" Bobbie screamed. "This can't be happening. I need my dad. Please, you have to go back in there and save him. Please." Scott grabbed Bobbie and held her in his lap while they both sobbed in each other's arms.

After a while, Bobbie fell asleep in Scott's arms and he gently sat her down in the chair. He walked in the hallway to call the ranch and tell them the news. Then he quietly went back to Lionel's room and held his hand as he cried for the loss of his father. There was a knock on the door letting him know that they needed to take him down to the morgue now.

"No, just give his family a few more minutes to come say good-bye. I'll let you know when we are ready." The nurse agreed and gave her sympathies for his loss. Soon the majority of the ranch was there to say their goodbyes. Scott allowed the nurse to take Lionel's body and then they headed home. It was a quiet ride and nobody talked. Scott and Bobbie had Tank drive them and a ranch hand drove Scott's truck back.

When they got to the ranch, Tank placed a hand on Scott's shoulder and gave him a look that let him know he was there for him. Scott walked Bobbie inside and when they got to their rooms, he pulled her over to his.

"I just need to hold you, please." Bobbie walked into his room and they both laid down. "I'm sorry you lost your father just as you got to meet him." Bobbie was silently crying.

"Why does it hurt so much? I mean I just met him, but I feel like I knew him my whole life. I don't know if it was better meeting him and losing him or if it would have been better to never know. I don't even know what I'm saying. I'm sorry. I'm just so lost right now." Scott scooted over to hold Bobbie even closer.

"I understand. I really do and I am so sorry." Bobbie and Scott just laid there holding each other.

"Would you tell me some more stories about him?" She asked after a few moments.

"Sure." Scott told a few of his favorites.

"He really was a great father, wasn't he?' Scott could only nod over the lump in his throat as the reality of the situation sunk in. Lionel was gone. "I feel like I should be consoling you."

"We can console each other." Scott tightened his arms around her.

"Why did this have to happen?" She sounded on the verge of tears again.

"I know. It's really not fair." Scott soothed, rubbing her back. He continued while she softly sobbed against his chest. She looked up at him with tear filled eyes and he couldn't resist pressing his lips to hers. He took advantage of her surprised gasp to slip his tongue inside to swirl with hers. He kissed her for several minutes; softly, slowly, and thoroughly exploring her mouth until she was moaning and clutching him tightly.

Bobbie couldn't believe this was happening or how good and right it felt. In her limited experience, she had never been kissed like this before. Bruce had been a sloppy kisser and the few boys before him hadn't had a clue what they were doing. But this man could seriously kiss and it was making her head spin.

"Wow." She breathed out when he finally pulled just milli-meters away.

"I'm sorry." Scott stroked the side of her face. "I shouldn't have done that. I just…"

"Yes you should have." Bobbie pulled him down into a gentle kiss, which Scott soon took control of. It ignited a flame in her that was almost boiling over. Over and over and over he gave her deep drugging kisses. She was all but to the point where she couldn't remember her own name.

"We should stop." Scott panted.

"Why?" That was the last thing Bobbie wanted

"Because." He pulled her on top of him, their bodies pressed flush and he kissed her again. "I want you so badly I can't stand it." He kissed her one last time. "I need a very cold shower." He said, attempting to rise. Bobbie didn't budge.

"Kiss me again." She said.

"Bobbie." He whispered. "Are you sure?"

"I'm sure." She pressed their lips together.

"I don't want you to feel like I'm taking advantage of your grief. I don't want this to be something you regret in the morning. I don't ever want you to think of this as a mistake."

"I would never regret this." Another scalding kiss and his hand moved to the hem of her shirt where his fingers slipped under to caress the soft skin of her stomach.

"Can we take this off?" At her nod, her tee shirt was slowly pulled over her head. Scott yanked his off in a more hurried fashion, desperate to feel her skin against his. His hand came up to cup and tease her breast through her bra while he kissed down her neck, paying special attention to the spot behind her ear that made her shiver. "Scott, I have to tell you something." She panted.

"You're a virgin? Please tell me you're not a virgin." He asked almost in a desperate plea. "I don't think I can be that gentle. "

"No, not a virgin. But I don't really have a lot of experience."

"We don't have to do anything." He said even though he was hard and aching.

"No I want this I just don't know if I will know what to do. I have only had sex like two times and both times he just pumped a few times and it was over. But I want this." She turned scarlet and looked away before she whispered.

Scott kissed her again, deep and intense, while thoughts raced through his mind. How could any man have his hands on her and not worship her? A couple of pumps, what a joke. But he guessed he could understand a little, just holding her he was having to hold back. He wanted her just as badly as she wanted him. He moved his hands to the button of her jeans and unfastened them. Slowly he began to pull them down her legs, she helped him out by lifting her hips at the right time, until she was in nothing but a matching bra and panty set.

"God Bobbie. You're perfect." She blushed again as Scott ridded himself of his own jeans and climbed back on top of her. But not before she clearly saw the outline of his large manhood beneath the blue boxer briefs he wore. Her look turned worried. "What's wrong?"

"Well." Her face was the color of a tomato. "You're really big and…" She trailed off, turning away.

"It'll be okay. I promise." He resumed kissing her neck while he deftly unhooked her bra and slid it down her shoulders.

"Ohh." Bobbie bit her lip and closed her eyes as his thumb rolled over her bare nipple. He trailed kisses down her neck until he reached her chest where his mouth replaced his hand. She moaned and squirmed as he licked and sucked at her sensitive flesh. The shy part of her wanted to stop; she hadn't even known Scott that long. The other part wanted nothing more than for this to continue; she'd never been more turned on in her life.

"Let me make you feel good baby." Scott scooted lower, hooking his thumbs in the sides of her underwear and started peeling them down. He encouraged her to spread her thighs then shifted his body so that his mouth lined up with her most intimate area. Bobbie's breath caught in her throat when his tongue glided over her outer folds.

"Oh god!" She cried out when he began exploring her thoroughly, commiting to memory every action that made her moan or squirm. Finally he came to the tight little bundle of throbbing nerves and took it into his mouth. "Scott!" He worshiped her flesh, mouth on her pleasure center while his hands gently roamed her body. Bobbie's brain turned to mush, her entire focus was on Scott and what he was doing to her. "Scott, oh my god, something's happening. I feel so… I'm not sure what…" She whispered. His fingers found her nipples again and that was it. "Scott!" She cried out when her orgasm hit, throwing her head back and curling her toes.

"So beautiful." Scott watched her for a moment; her eyes were closed, her jaw was slack, and she was breathing like she'd just run a marathon. And there was this look on her face; it was an intense look of awe, pleasure, and satisfaction. He felt like a god for having been the one to put it there.

"I've never…" She lay there panting, her head spinning barely able to open her eyes.

"Never what baby?" He asked, kissing her again.

"Felt like that."

"You've never had an orgasm?" He asked incredulously.

"Not really." She whispered shyly.

"Surly by yourself though." She shook her head, looking away and turning even redder.

"Sometimes after he finished, I'd try to get myself there, but it never felt anything like that." Her face was flaming by this point. He'd never wanted someone so badly in his life, but he had to be sure Bobbie was still on board.

"Are you still sure? We can stop now if you want."

"I don't want to stop. Especially if you can make me feel like that again." She whispered, her eyes fluttering open and locking with his. "I want you Scott."

"Thank god. Trust me if you thought that felt good, you're gonna love what comes next." He moved back up to kiss her as he rummaged through his bedside table for a condom. Scott pulled away and rose to his knees. He ripped the condom open with his teeth and quickly rolled it down his shaft. "I need you." Slowly sank into her hot, wet, and extremely tight passage. "Bobbie." He breathed out.

"Scott." She felt so full.

"Just relax baby." Scott leaned down and took her mouth again. He ran his hands gently up and down her body as they kissed. After a while, he pulled back to look into her eyes; they were dilated and full of desire once again. Scott smiled and set up a slow steady rhythm for them. He angled his hips in different ways until he found one that had her crying out his name.

"Scott." She moaned. Bobbie couldn't believe how good this felt; she'd never known such pleasure existed. But she needed more somehow. She wrapped her legs around his waist and rocked her hips in sync with his, but she needed more. "Scott, please." She whispered, voice wrecked. "I need…" She trailed off, having no idea what to ask for.

"I know what you need." He said, increasing his pace and she moaned out her approval.

"Oh god yes." Bobbie panted. "Like that. More. Please."

The sound of the beautiful woman underneath him begging for him was almost more than he could take. The feeling of her around him was already driving him crazy. His strokes sped up, trying to give her what she desired, but that put him on the edge way too quickly.

"Scott." She whimpered, she was so close again. He took her mouth in a deep passionate kiss and that was all it took. Bobbie closed her eyes as her world exploded around her.

Bobbie coming apart beneath him was his undoing. Feeling her tighten and pulse around him caused his control to snap. His thrusts became more erratic and, after only a few more, he joined her in bliss.

"God Bobbie." He breathed out, resting his forehead against hers for a moment.

"Is it always that good? Man I can't believe what I was missing out on."

"No baby, it has never really been that good for me either." He'd never felt this close to another person. Scott rolled away to dispose of the condom and then was tugging her back into his arms, fingers gliding over the bare skin of her back. They said nothing for a long while. "We should talk about this." He finally whispered, but heard her breathing even out and knew that she was asleep. They could deal with this tomorrow, right now he needed to hold her. It had been a long and trying day, they both needed sleep. He kissed the top of her head, pulled her more securely against him, and closed his eyes.

A few hours later, Scott woke up and watched Bobbie sleep for a few minutes before he gently woke her up.

"We need to wake up and get ready to make funeral arrangements. Then I'll try to call Mr. Bradshaw one more time. Why not see if Lynn can come to Texas? I would be happy to pay for her ticket." Scott and Bobbie got up, showered, and got ready.

CHAPTER 12

On the way to the funeral home Bobbie did call Lynn to tell her she needed her. Lynn hung up and called her dad.

"Daddy, I need to use the private plane. Bobbie is in Texas and she needs me. She just lost her dad." Lynn got ready and her father picked her up to drive her to the plane himself. As she entered, her father was right behind her. "What are you doing? I've ridden by myself plenty of times."

"Yes you have and I see no problem with that, however, I want to be there for Bobbie as well. Do you mind if we share a plane ride?"

"Oh Daddy, I love you." They made the ride to Texas and had a car waiting for them.

"Okay so where are we going?" Peter Daniels asked his daughter.

"Oh God! I was in such a hurry to get here that I didn't even ask. Let me call her." Lynn pulled out her phone and called Bobbie. There was no answer. She tried again and again no answer. Her father asked for any information she might have. "I know he has a ranch, I know his first name is Lionel. Oh wait, Bobbie said Lionel James with the LJ Ranch. Yes, his initials."

"Take us to the LJ Ranch please." Peter told his driver.

"I can't believe that you're here with me."

"Lynn, baby she's your best friend and has been for many years. She knows how much money you have and yet she refuses to take any from you. I know you have offered help many times and she refused to take your help. I also know when you needed her she has dropped everything and been there for you. I love Bobbie for who she is. Now it's time to show her we are here for her." Lynn and Peter rode the rest of the way in quiet, just thinking about their lives. The car pulled up to the ranch and they were surprised by how many people were there. They got out and Peter walked up to the first person he saw. "Hello, I'm Peter Daniels. We are from Colorado to show our support for Bobbie Lahey. Do you know where we can find her?"

"Name's Tank, I help run this ranch. It's nice to meet you. Bobbie is with Scott down at the funeral parlor making the arrangements as we speak. They should be here within the hour. Come on over and have a seat. We're all just waiting for word." Tank led Lynn and Peter to a couple of chairs.

Lynn was so heartbroken for her friend that she didn't even notice the sexy ranch hands looking at her. Randy sat down next to her and introduced himself. He then told stories about Bobbie on the ranch.

"You should have seen her try to get on a horse for the first time. Bobbie was scared of horses since she hadn't been around them. They can be intimidating due to their size, but they are actually really gentle. Mr. Daniels would you and your daughter like a tour of the ranch? I would be happy to give you a little tour while we wait." Peter agreed and all three of them headed to the barn first. "This is Tex. This is the horse Scott had Bobbie get on the first time.

"This is like the biggest horse I see here." Lynn called out.

"Yes Ma'am, it is. We usually start newbies on Dreamsicle over here." Randy walked over to Dreamsicle and gave her a sugar cube. "I think Scott took a quick liking to Bobbie and was trying to make a play. If she was scared then she would have to hold on. Scott's not the kind of guy that plays around with girls' hearts. Mr.

James was an honest man and he expected that from his workers. We only have maybe one or two that we call players. They are still sort of new to the ranch and haven't learned yet. They do seem to be slowing down on that. Let me show you the ranch." They walked up the stairs in the back of the barn and walked out onto a balcony of sorts. "From here you can see most of the land. I love to come up here and think. The land is so beautiful." Randy pointed to the east and showed them the J&R Ranch. Then to the west there wasn't a neighbor in sight.

"So how many acres are on this ranch?" Peter asked.

"I'd say close to five thousand." Both Lynn and Peter blew out a whistle at that number.

"Wow." Was all Lynn could say.

Down below Denise was walking out with a huge tray of sandwiches and bags of chips.

"COME AND GET IT." Randy walked Peter and Lynn back down and they sat around and ate. Many stories were told about Lionel and Scott. Tank started the stories.

"Do y'all remember when Scott came to the ranch? That was a smart mouth kid if I ever saw one. For those of you who weren't here, let me tell you. Scott was a stringy little guy. His cast probably weighed more than him. I was told that I had to train him on a horse. Before his cast came off, I had to get him comfortable with being near a horse. The first day he gets here Lionel walks out to meet him. He explains he's welcome and then after he heals up he will have to help out around the ranch. Do you know what his reaction was? That scrawny little thing looked up at Lionel and said "I'm not cleaning out any horse shit." Everyone started laughing.

Then more stories were told about how Lionel helped each of them. The newest guy, Frank, said that when he got hired he went out to celebrate. He might have had a little too much to drink and ended up in jail. Lionel came and bailed him out and told him next time not to drink so much. Then he never brought it up again.

"What kind of boss bails you out of jail on your first day and doesn't say anything?" All the ranch hands just quietly shook their heads and mumbled.

"Lionel."

Two hours later, a truck pulled into the driveway and Scott got out; he walked over to open Bobbie's door. As soon as she stepped onto the ground, Lynn was racing toward her.

"Oh my God! Bobbie! How are you? Are you okay? Do you need anything?" Lynn was squeezing Bobbie so tight.

"Put me down you Amazon woman." Bobbie joked with Lynn. "I can't believe you're here. When did your flight land? We could have picked you up." Behind Lynn Bobbie caught sight of Peter walking toward them. Bobbie ran up to him and gave him a tight hug.

"I'm sorry to hear about your father, sweetie. If there's anything I can do, please let me know. Lynn and I'll be around a few days if you need us."

"Thank you, I can't believe you're here. I know how busy you are."

"I'm never too busy for you. Always remember that." Bobbie introduced Peter and Lynn to Scott.

"This is my best friend who is more like a sister, Lynn Daniels. This is Mr. Daniels who has always been there for me growing up." Scott reached out and shook hands with Peter. He reached for Lynn and pulled her into a hug.

"Lionel really loved you. Whenever he would talk to you on the phone, he always had a huge smile. I'm so sorry that you two couldn't meet in person." Lynn's eyes got watery as she explained that she was trying to set things up to come visit.

"But when Bobbie called I just left everything. I told Dad I needed his plane and we left. I guess I should make some calls. Later." They both chuckled and walked to the rest of the group so Scott could explain everything. Scott again grabbed Bobbie's hand and addressed the crowd.

"Old Man will be buried on Friday. He has a spot he wanted to be buried here on the land. It's under that old oak, way in the back quarter. Tank, Randy, Frank, Ted, Kyle Bradshaw and I will act as pallbearers. I was told to ask if anyone wants to say a few words; let me know so I can put your name down. Does anyone have any questions?" No one had any and when they were done all the ranch hands got up and grabbed a shovel and headed to the back quarter to start to dig. No one said anything, but everyone felt it. Peter got up and grabbed a shovel and followed along.

"You don't have to do this." Bobbie ran up to him.

"He was your father and I love you. I'm doing this for you." Bobbie sat back down with tears in her eyes. She looked over at Lynn who was also crying. "I can't believe your dad would do something like this for me." Lynn gave her a tight hug.

"Our dad is doing this for you. I have told you for many years he loves you like his own daughter. Some of the time I think he likes you more." Both girls laughed quietly.

"Sorry to interrupt." Denise came up to them. "But I made up the guest room upstairs and I'll give my room to Mr. Daniels. Since we're engaged now, I suppose it's time I start living with Tank."

"I didn't know you were engaged." Lynn jumped up. "Why did you not tell me?" Denise and Bobbie laughed at Lynn's excitement. It was hard to remember that Lynn never actually met these people, but she felt connected through the stories told by Bobbie. Denise showed her the ring and explained how it all happened. Then they all got sad again when they realized that was the last time they all saw Lionel.

The men came back one by one and put up the shovels, then left to be alone. Lynn had followed Randy with her eyes. When she saw him go to the barn, she chose to follow him. Lionel was more than just a boss to many of these men and she wanted to see if she could do anything for Randy. The last two men walking back were Scott and Peter. With how Peter was pointing to various parts of the land, it looked as if he was trying to learn things about the ranch. Scott was happy to tell him about everything. As they entered the barn the Bobbie could hear Peter say to Scott.

"I heard about this horse you put my Bobbie on. Is there a reason you chose not to use a smaller, gentler horse?" Both men laughed, but Scott never answered.

The three of them went into the house and Bobbie told Peter that he could stay in Denise's old room since she was moving. To keep busy, most of the ranch hands helped Denise carry her things, except the bed and dresser since she wouldn't need them, out to Tank's cottage, and thanks to all the activity, no one noticed Lynn's lengthy absence.

A few hours later, the community got word of what happened and came to offer condolences and help. Bobbie sat there and drank in every story anyone wanted to share about her dad. Even old man Henderson came by and shared a few stories of his own. Late that night Kyle Bradshaw showed up with tears streaming down his face.

"I'm so sorry. I just got all my messages. I was on a cruise and didn't have reception. I would have swum back if I had to. Lionel was my best friend. I'm so sorry." He was facing more toward Scott, but then he looked around and when he saw Bobbie he gasped. "Oh my Lord, you really are his daughter. If I didn't know any better, I would have sworn you were his twin. Look at you. You have the same eyes and the same nose. Oh please excuse my manners. My name is Kyle Bradshaw. I'm your father's lawyer as well as his best friend." Bobbie walked over and gave Kyle a hug.

"Nice to meet you, this is my best friend from Colorado, Lynn Daniels and her father Peter Daniels." Peter stood and shook hands with Kyle, as did Lynn, then they all sat down again.

"What exactly happened?" Kyle asked and Scott started telling the story.

"We were working on the roof and he fell. I called 9-1-1 and they took him straight to the hospital. He had a broken leg and a broken rib that punctured his lung. If it wasn't for that, I'm not sure we would have ever known. As he was recovering I decided to go ahead and finish the remodel of the kitchen and that is when I found the letter telling him about Bobbie." Scott walked over to the table and showed the letter to Peter and Kyle who were sitting next to each other. He gave a look to Lynn.

"I would show you but I'm sure you already know what it says." He told her. Lynn just smiled and shook her head in agreement. Scott continued. "I went online and found three possibilities for Allison Lahey. Having seen a picture I knew the other two women were not his Ally. I then read the obituary with the survivor of Bobbie Jean Lahey. I flew up to Colorado and explained to Bobbie what was happening and then left telling her I was leaving a ticket for her. I can't believe how rude I was. I never took into consideration that she might not want to meet Old Man. I just knew he would have wanted to know her and I would have done anything for him."

"Yeah, you were not the nicest guy that day." Bobbie laughed a little. " You never even gave me a chance to ask questions and you didn't give me any information, besides his name. I'm so glad that I decided to get on that plane."

"Excuse me." Lynn cleared her throat loudly. "Why did you get on that plane? Oh yeah, I made you." Bobbie rolled her eyes at Lynn and agreed that yes, Lynn had a lot to do with it.

After a couple more stories, Kyle left and the rest made their way to their rooms. Once upstairs, Bobbie found herself in a slightly awkward place. Did she sleep with Lynn in the guest room or with Scott again in his room? Scott didn't even give her a choice.

"Night Lynn, we'll see you in the morning."

"Goodnight." Lynn shot Bobbie a knowing smile and a wink, which made her blush.

"Goodnight." Bobbie echoed. Then Scott grabbed her by the hand and led her into his room.

"Is this okay? I just really need you right now." Bobbie shook her head yes. Scott took her into his arms, mouth finding hers, as soon as the door closed behind them. Bobbie clung to him, his strong arms around her making her feel safe even as his lips brushing against hers dialed up the heat.

"Don't want to think about anything but you." He whispered truthfully when the kiss finally broke.

Bobbie nodded her agreement before kissing him again. She didn't want to think about today either; not about the father she had just lost or the arrangements they'd had to make, not about her best friend just down the hall and what she might be thinking about them. She wanted to lose herself in Scott. Wanted nothing more than for him to make her feel incredible again. But it was more than that. She needed to be as close as possible to him; needed his warmth, and strength, and comfort. And she longed to provide him with those same things.

"Kick off your boots." He told her before bringing her to his bed and laying down at her side, kissing her until her head began to swim with desire. Needing to be even closer, Bobbie pushed at his shoulder until he rolled to his back and then she straddled his waist. Scott let out a hiss of breath when her bottom brushed his hardness and he started rocking against her. They stayed that way for endless minutes, making out while they grinded together, until they were both panting.

"Scott." She whispered, sitting up. "I want to make you feel good."

"Then kiss me again." He told her.

She started with his lips, placing a gentle kiss on them before moving to his jawline and down his neck, pausing to pull his shirt over his head then remove her own.

"Bobbie." He moaned while she explored his chest with her mouth. She shifted to kneel between his thighs then trailed her tongue down past his navel to the waistband of the jeans he wore. Her hands shook slightly as she brought them up to undo the button and slide the zipper down. "Fuck." He murmured when her small hand brushed his rigid cock. He had a feeling what she was going to do and the thought of her mouth on him caused him to harded further. He felt the tug as she attempted to pull his pants and boxer briefs down and helped her by shoving them off. Bobbie looked up at him with a shy smile as her soft hands ran up and down his shaft causing his eyes to flutter shut for a second. He pulled her down into a deep kiss.

"I've never done this before." She said timidly, rising back to her knees and stroking him more deliberately, with a little more of a rhythm.

"You don't have to." Scott managed to make himself say despite how badly he wanted this.

"But I really, really want to." She bent to swipe her tongue across the head, the taste of his precome instantly coating it. He jerked and moaned loudly.

"Oh my god, I'm so sorry…" Bobbie started to apologize and pulled her hand away, thinking she'd done something wrong.

"No baby, you're doing great. That feels so good." Scott replaced her hand and moaned again when she continued stroking. "Just a little tighter baby." Bobbie tightened her grip and found she really liked the sound of his moans and wanted to hear more of them.

"God." He breathed out when she did it again, more confidently this time. "Bobbie, please." He begged when he could no longer take her teasing tongue along his shaft, she was driving him out of his mind with need. "Fuck." He breathed heavily as she took him into her mouth and began to suck. "Bobbie." He panted. "Harder baby." She complied. "God. Just like that." The feeling of her hot, wet mouth around him left him unable to think about anything else, so he closed his eyes and let the pleasure wash over him. When he opened them again, he found Bobbie looking up at him, eyes dark and full of desire. He couldn't wait any longer to be inside of her. "Need you baby."

Bobbie was loving every minute of this and every sound of pleasure that he made turned her on more. It was heady to know that she could push him to his limits. Part of her didn't want to stop, wanted to see if she could make him lose control like this. Instead of answering him, she continued until she heard him growl. He grabbed her and hauled her up his body into a blistering kiss. Somehow, without ever breaking the kiss, he managed to find a condom and put it on.

"Want you on top." His voice was a little strained as he guided her into position. With one hand, he held himself steady, while the other was on her side. She sank all the way down until their hips were flush. He pulled her down into a kiss.

"I'm not sure what to do." Her own breathing was heavy, the feeling of fullness overwhelming her again.

"Just do whatever feels good baby." Experimentally she rocked her hips and damn that was good, so she kept it up. "That's it baby." Both hands went to her waist to help her slide up and down his cock. And holy hell did that feel even better. When she would have increased her speed, Scott stilled her. "Nice and slow." If he went fast, there was no way he would last long. They kept his maddenly glacial pace until Bobbie was bucking against his grasp; her orgasm so close. If only he would move faster.

"Scott, please." She begged.

"Ready to go faster?" Inside he was just as strung out as she was. He'd had to go over payroll and taxes just to keep from coming the moment he got inside of her. He relaxed his hold on her, allowing her the freedom to speed up.

"Scott." God she was beautiful above him, head thrown back in pleasure. Eventually the need for control got the better of him and his grip tightened again, urging her on faster and faster. "Scott."

"Bobbie." He moaned as they managed a simultaneous orgasm. She quivered and collapsed on top of him while he trembled from the force of it, holding her tight. "Every time with you is just so completely amazing, I can't get enough of you." Scott whispered in her ear.

"I know what you mean." She'd never felt this close to another person. She was falling for Scott and that scared the shit out of her. What if he didn't feel the same way? Scott disposed of the condom then came back to take her into his arms. "Scott, I…" She began, but then he yawned. "We should get some sleep." She said instead. "We have a long day ahead of us tomorrow."

"Yeah." Scott agreed, arranging them so that her head was on his chest. "Goodnight baby." He murmured.

Bobbie lay awake long after he had fallen asleep. Her mind was running with everything. Mostly with how fast she was starting to have feelings for Scott. She wasn't the kind of girl to just sleep around. What if he was only using her while she was here? After hours of tossing and turning Bobbie finally was able to fall asleep.

CHAPTER 13

The day of the funeral the house was quiet as everyone was thinking about Lionel.

Scott was thinking about the many years he had come to love the Old Man and how much his life had improved. He wondered what would have happened to him had Lionel not accepted him.

Bobbie was thinking about how much she had missed out on not knowing her father sooner. She hated to put blame on her mother, but she was the only person who knew everything. She wondered what her mother's reasons were. She couldn't see any reason as to why you would keep your child away from their other parent. If Lionel had been abusive or mean, she would have understood, but all the stories she heard were about how great he was. He would give you the shirt off his back if you needed it. Bobbie heard stories about how her mother never needed or wanted for anything because Lionel would get it for her.

Lynn was in the next room feeling bad for her friend. She couldn't imagine losing her daddy. She wondered if Bobbie would be coming back to Colorado at all. She noticed the hand holding and the looks that Bobbie and Scott shot each other, then there was the fact that they were sleeping together. What would she do without her best friend and sister if Bobbie decided to stay? She really seemed at home on this gorgeous ranch. Her thoughts shifted to one particularly gorgeous thing on the ranch; Randy. He was sweet, fun, and oh my god hot. She quickly pushed those thoughts away. She was here for Bobbie and, today especially, Lynn needed to keep it all about her.

Down stairs Peter was thinking about Bobbie and how she never showed signs of needing help even when he knew that she needed it. He loved her as his own and would always help her when he could. He prayed that she would be okay during the funeral.

Outside the ranch hands were discussing their futures. They were not sure what would happen to the land or their jobs. Three had already applied to work on other ranches and one was considering leaving town. Tank and Denise were trying to calm them all down and explained that Lionel had taken care of them; just to be calm and patient.

The morning came too early for Scott and Bobbie, who decided to go to the funeral home early to double check everything was set up and ready to go. They talked to the preacher about who was going to speak. So far they had Tank, Denise, and three ranch hands who wanted to. Scott told him that after those five had a chance to speak, he should ask the guests if anyone wanted to say anything. As they made their way back into the chapel, they told him about how Lionel came to find out about Bobbie and how Scott and Bobbie would share the land and continue on in Lionel's memory.

As they were talking, Tank and Denise walked in. They apologized for being so early, but they knew the chapel would fill up fast and they wanted to sit close to Lionel. After giving Scott and Bobbie a hug each they shook the hand of the preacher and then asked if there was anything they could do.

Once they were sitting down in the second pew, the door opened again. This time Lynn and Peter walked in. Peter walked right up to Bobbie and pulled her into a long, tight hug.

"I'm here for you baby girl. I'll always be here for you. Just say the word and I'm there. Not just today but always, do you get me?" Peter looked into Bobbie's tear filled eyes. She had a huge lump in her throat so she only nodded and hugged Peter harder. "Oh and because I want to prove that I can take care of you, look here." Peter pulled out four packets of tissues and handed one to Bobbie. "There are more where those came from baby girl."

Lynn gently pushed her father out of the way so she could give Bobbie hugs and Peter moved over to gently give Scott a hug with a handshake. Lynn asked Bobbie if there was anything she could do to help.

"You being here is helpful enough. I love you Lynn. I know you are busy and your dad is busy. I hate that you're here for me when you should be back in Colorado. However, I'm so thankful that you are both here. I need you here. I love you Lynn." They both grabbed each other for a big hug.

"Always sister, I will always be here."

Just then the door opened and Randy and a couple of ranch hands came in. Lynn and Peter found a seat near the front to be able to be close to Bobbie. Randy gave both Scott and Bobbie a hug. He asked if there was anything that needed to be done. As he waited for the other ranch hands to give their condolences he casually looked around the chapel to see if Lynn was there yet. There was some kind of attraction with her he hadn't felt in such a long time. He shook his head to erase where his mind was going. Today was a day for Lionel.

Pretty soon the door was held open as many of the members of the community had come to pay their respects. Scott introduced Bobbie to a few of them as they came through the line. A couple of whispers were heard about how no one knew of a daughter, but Bobbie ignored those comments. No one knew their story and it was no one's business but hers and Lionel's. During a small gap between the groups of people paying their respects, Scott inhaled deeply which got Bobbie's attention. Scott walked over to a lady and she followed.

"What do you think you are doing here Betty? I told you that I was not ready to have you in my life. What makes you think I would want to see you today, of all days?" Scott asked quietly, but there was anger in his voice. Bobbie grabbed his hand to try to calm him down.

"I understand how you feel Scott, trust me I do. I didn't come here to get you upset. I only came here to see if there was anything I could do for you. I also came to pay my respects to Mr. James. He was there for you when I should have been. I know he was more of a parent to you than I ever was..." Scott interrupted her by slightly raising his voice

"DAMN RIGHT he was more of a parent. He protected me when you hid in the next room. He showed me respect when you did nothing but belittle me. He showed me unconditional love when you showed me hate, despair, and violence. That is something I'll never forgive you for." Before he could finish, Tank pulled him away and into a private room.

"I got you boy. Let it out. You have been holding that in for a long ass time. Go ahead, let it out." Tank quietly held Scott in a bear hug as Scott sobbed into Tank's shoulders. Outside the room Bobbie quietly thanked Betty for coming.

"I understand that you've changed your life. I, for one, am proud of you for that. I know how hard it's to make changes. However, you need to realize that Scott was hurt in more ways than one with the life you allowed him to be brought up in. I don't have any children, but I promise you that no one would ever lay a finger on them and live. I don't know your story and maybe one day we can meet on better terms, but for now please find a seat and allow Scott to grieve in his own way." Betty apologized for making a scene and quietly found a pew in the back.

A little while later, Tank and Scott walked out of the room. Tank went straight back to sit next to Denise and Scott gave Bobbie a hug.

"I'm so sorry for that. I can't believe I made such a big deal about her coming. I guess I should have expected her to come if she's trying to be in my life again. I don't know what came over me. Please understand I would normally never cause a scene like that, especially when we are here for Old Man." Scott was clearly upset and the only thing Bobbie could think of was to give him a hug.

"It's okay Scott. I understand. It sounded like you really needed to get that off your chest and I'm sure that Daddy would have been proud." They squeezed each other a little tighter and then moved to welcome the rest of the guests into the chapel. The preacher acknowledged it was time to start, so Bobbie and Scott found their seats. As they were passing by Lynn and Peter, Bobbie grabbed their hands and brought them to sit with her. Scott squeezed Tank's shoulder in a silent way of saying thanks. Scott, Bobbie, Lynn and Peter were sitting in the front row when the preacher thanked everyone for coming and started the funeral.

"Dearly beloved, we are gathered here today to say goodbye to Mr. Lionel James. He was a father, a friend, and a boss. But to those of us who really knew him he was so much more. In all my years as Lionel's friend I have never heard anything bad about him. In my line of work you can imagine the stories I hear. In each case about Lionel was about him being giving, caring, loving and just such a blessing. I'm going to open the podium for some of you to share your thoughts and stories with the rest of us but before I do, may I share a story of my own? Ten years ago we had some vandalism done to my church. We fundraised and asked for money. To be honest we were not above begging at that moment. I was out one day walking the streets and asking anyone for any loose change so that we could rebuild our church. You see the vandalism damage was a hole in the roof so they could access the building, then they stole the copper from our ac units, they took every electronic we had in the building and they broke into the safe and took all the money. Not that the church had a lot to start with. Well I decided to take a break and go into Pop's Diner. I was seated towards the back and the waitress asked me how things were going. I don't know why but I told her about my problems. I placed my order and she left. I was sitting there trying to think of what else we could do to raise the funds. As I was deep in thought, a man came over to introduce himself as Mr. Lionel James and asked if he could join me. He asked if the vandals were ever caught and charged. I replied that they had not and we got to talking about what had happened and the damage it caused. We discussed the amount of money it would take to even start to rebuild. I explained that I just wanted to fix the roof and the ac so my congregation had a safe place to meet. We made small talk as our orders came out. He was nice enough to pay for my meal and then he thanked me for taking time to just talk to him. I went about my day and started to ask more people for money. I did get some, however not enough to make a difference. I went to bed that night and prayed for some help. The next morning I went to church to try to gather up my congregation to come up with any other ideas. I was surprised to see some men working on my roof. I asked the guy in charge what was going on- I couldn't afford to fix the roof. As I was talking to him a van pulled in and started to work on my air conditioner. He explained that the one I had was a little too small for the building and he would put in a bigger unit and make sure I had the proper ductwork for each room. I stopped him to explain that I couldn't afford to pay him, but he just smiled and walked away. I was turning in circles trying to figure out what was happening. A short time later a bus pulled up with a bunch of the high school kids each holding different types of electronics. Some had computers and laptops, some had stereos, others had surround sound equipment and then they started to set it all up. A guy walked up to me and asked where my safe was. I pointed him to the room it was supposed to be in and explained that they stole it right out of the closet. He said that he was going to put in a newer model that went into the wall and was fireproof. Late that night I had a new church. Some of the congregation heard what was happening and they came and worked in the church yard, and painted some of the older rooms. It was not until months later I learned that Mr. James was the one who paid for everything. I went to ask him why he would do something like that when he didn't even know me. His reply was God Bless you. As some of you may know my church took him into our hearts that day. My congregation wanted to do something for him. However, if you knew Mr. James, you knew he was more of a giver than a taker. So my church started a scholarship foundation for local seniors. It's the Lionel James Scholarship. As I said he was a giver so instead of simply taking the honor he chose to continue to give ten thousand dollars every year. Mr. James will be greatly missed." Choking up the preacher coughed a few times and then continued. "I'm sorry; it's such an honor to be able to lead you in a funeral for such a great man. Tank, I believe you had a few words to say? Come on up." Tank thanked the preacher and turned to the guests.

"Lionel was a smart mouth little punk that thought he could get away with anything he wanted." He started. "As young boys growing up, Lionel thought he was so much better since his father had a ranch. As a teen he was not much better to be honest. Although instead of his dad having a ranch, Lionel used his looks to get whatever he wanted. Once Lionel left for college, I applied to be a ranch hand since I figured I wouldn't have to see him much. However, when Lionel was nineteen and his parents were killed in a driving accident, he changed overnight. He apologized for his attitude growing up and we became close. Lionel did a lot of good for the community. He never treated anyone as anything but equal when you worked with him." Tank looked over at the casket. "I'll miss you, my friend." Tank sat down and Denise held him as he quietly cried into her hair.

Randy got up and introduced himself. "I came from Montana where my family had a ranch. It wasn't as big as the LJ ranch, but it was a good size. I was an ungrateful teenager who thought a girl was more important than my family and I followed her here to Texas. Choosing her over my family, they disowned me. Within a year she had cheated on me and was pregnant. I went home early one day to have all my stuff boxed up. She didn't even give me a chance to look for a place to sleep. I went back to work to the gas station to ask a coworker if I could sleep on their couch only to learn I had a two day suspension. So I was really in a tough spot. Lionel overheard my arguing with the manager and took me to his ranch. He put me to work and he helped me reconnect with my family. The day I started on his ranch, we found out that my dad was in the hospital, dying. He flew me to Montana and, when my dad passed, he paid for his funeral and made sure my family had all the financial help they needed. I mean I only knew of Mr. James as a customer at the convenience store and met him one day and he did all this for me. I still talk to my family weekly and visit about twice a year. All because a stranger cared." Randy looked up towards the ceiling. " I'll miss you Lionel. Thank you for everything." Randy went back to his pew and sat quietly thinking about all that Lionel did for him.

One by one a few ranch hands came up to talk about how he had gone above and beyond being a boss. The preacher called out to the guests to ask if anyone else had anything to say. One lady, Penelope, walked to the podium.

"Hello all, you all know who I am. I own Pop's Diner. What can I say about Lionel? Well he was special all right. He had his booth in the back so he could see everything. He liked to know what was going on with everyone. Very few people pay attention the way he did. If he heard of someone needing anything, he tried to get them help. He heard of a little boy who needed a home and took him in. The problem was, it was supposed to be temporary, however when he was supposed to go back Lionel had a fit and held onto the boy as if he were his own son. Scott, I know you know this already but let me tell you. That man loved you like his own son. He would brag about all the smallest or the biggest things you did. Bobbie, I know that you just found out that Lionel was your daddy. I'm so glad that you got the chance to at least meet the man. He was a great man and we all loved him dearly. I'm sorry for both of your losses." Penelope walked back to her seat and more people came to talk about Lionel. His funeral went on for hours with everyone wanting to share how Lionel touched their lives.

Once the last person was able to speak, they made their way to their cars as Tank, Randy, Frank, Ted, Kyle, and Scott all made their way to the front. Denise gave Tank a kiss and told him she would be waiting in the car for him. Peter held Bobbie's hand and walked her to Scott's car and then he and Lynn got in the back seat. Once the Pallbearers were in their vehicles the hearse drove through town towards the ranch where Lionel would be buried. Bobbie noticed how every store was closed with signs on the windows. As they slowed to turn a corner she read one of the signs: Closed for the funeral of Lionel James

"Everything is closed." She said with tears in her eyes.

"Pop's Diner has never been closed since I came to live here. When Penelope's own father died, she stayed open and went to the funeral. She just hired an extra waitress for the two days she was gone."

Hearing how sweet this town was made her tears flow down her cheeks faster. As she was staring off looking at what looked like a ghost town, Peter reached forward and handed her a tissue.

"See baby girl, I'll always look after you." All four of them started to laugh. It took awhile for everyone to park at the ranch and walk to his resting place. The rest of the funeral went smoothly with them praying over him and the lowering of his casket. Bobbie and Scott stayed until the last of the guests left and then each said their own goodbye. Lynn and Peter held back as well. When Bobbie was done she fell on her knees. She was sobbing out loud.

"Why? I just met him. Why would God take him from me? Now I have no one. I'm so alone now," Scott, Lynn and Peter all ran to her.

"No, you are not alone baby girl. We are all here for you. That's what we have been telling you for years." Peter was trying to calm her down as Lynn was rubbing her hair back the way her mother used to do when she was upset. Scott was just standing there telling her softly that she wasn't alone. He was there and her best friend and her father were there. She would never be alone.

A little while later Scott drove Peter back to his vehicle and they all made their way back to the house. Scott had Bobbie ride with him so she could gather her emotions before having to meet the people back at the house. There was no parking at the ranch, so Scott parked at the J&R Ranch next door and they took a golf cart to their ranch. Once inside they were bombarded with people. Some were openly crying, some were laughing, and some were just sitting quietly listening to the stories being told.

A few hours later, the last of the guests had left and Bobbie, Denise, and Lynn were in the kitchen trying to find room for all the food. They ended up sending most of it to the guy's cabins so it wouldn't go to waste. Then they all fell onto the couch and just sat there. They were all too tired to even try to talk, not that anyone had anything to say. It was getting late so Denise excused herself and went home. Lynn scooted closer to Bobbie.

"How are you feeling? If you even try to say fine, I'll slap you upside the head." They both laughed as Bobbie explained that she was feeling lost.

"All this time he was right here helping his community. I was asking my mom since I was little about my dad and she never told me. I could have been with him at least during the summers if my mom said something. Why would she hide him from me?" Lynn just held her tight as she let out all her frustrations. Once she calmed down, both women headed up the stairs to bed. As they crossed Scott's room he opened the door, pulled Bobbie in and told Lynn good night.

That night Bobbie and Scott talked about everything. They talked for hours. Scott told her about his mom and how he was thinking about meeting for coffee, but was still not sure. He told her about what he knew of his dad.

"Did you know he showed up today? He came in and sat in the back corner. He didn't say hi to me or my mom. My mother never even looked at him."

They talked a little about his thoughts on the "what if's" of his life. What if Lionel never took him in? What if the judge had made him go back to his dad full time when he was seventeen? What if he never found that note and came to get her? That last what if was a hard one to think about for both of them. She was thinking she would have never met her father and he was thinking that he would have never met her.

The next day was sad. Scott and Bobbie called all the ranch hands to a meeting. Scott took the lead on what to expect now that Lionel was gone.

"Look I know that some of you are nervous about your jobs now that Old Man is gone. I'll guarantee your job to you as long as you continue to work as hard as you have for him. Some of you have already put your resumes out there to work for other ranches. We're okay with that. If you would rather work for them, please feel free. However, if you leave and it doesn't work out, then you are more than welcome to come back. We'll find work for you. Just let us know if you're staying or going. No pressure. The Old Man left the ranch to Bobbie and me. If any of you will have trouble working for either of us, there's the road, see you later. That being said, I hope that we can get back to work as soon as possible. Tank, I'll be in the office for most of the week to get things caught up and organized. Would you be able to handle things or do you need me to stay out here?" Tank looked around and decided that he was going to handle things on his own for now, but that he would let him know. The meeting was closed and all the ranch hands went back to work. Scott and Bobbie went into the office to go through the paperwork that Lionel had, to see if they were caught up on their bills and if they needed to order supplies. As they were talking about ideas they had, they heard a knock on the door. One of the ranch hands, Steve, entered the room.

"Is this a bad time?" Steve asked.

"Nope you know we have an open door policy here. What can I do for you Steve?" Scott asked.

"When Lionel passed I wasn't sure of my future here." Steve wouldn't make eye contact. "So I went ahead and applied for a ranch a couple of towns over. I thought about it and decided that I'm going to take the job."

"That's too bad. You're a great worker Steve and we're gonna miss you. Is there anything we can do to make you stay?" Scott asked.

"No. Working on the ranch with Lionel gone would just be too hard." Steve again wouldn't make eye contact. "It's not that I have a problem with either of you as a boss. I just feel like it's my time to go." They talked about the new position at the new ranch and then Bobbie asked him when he was planning on leaving. "The sooner the better I think. Like I said, I applied a while ago."

"Okay, well after you are packed up and ready to go come see me and I'll give you your last check." Scott said. When Steve left to pack up Scott explained to Bobbie that Steve was a hard worker. "Did you know that he sends most of his checks to his mother to care for his younger sister? His sister has a disease that forces his mother to stay home to watch over her, and so money is tight with his family." Scott explained that he was going to give him some extra money and send his parents a check for ten thousand dollars. They both agreed and when Steve came to get his check he tried to hand it back to them.

"I can't take this money. I really do appreciate it, but all I need is what is owed to me."

"I was looking at the books and noticed that you haven't called in sick once since you started. The extra is just back pay." Bobbie explained. Steve was shocked and humbly accepted the check.

"Thank you both so much. Hey, were you serious about us being able to come back if it doesn't work out?" Asked Steve.

"Yes." Scott and Bobbie said at the same time. Steve nodded his head as he left the office. The rest of the day was spent talking and going over the papers in the office.

It was probably shortly after six o'clock when Kyle Bradshaw came knocking on their door. Lynn, Peter, and Bobbie were in the living room chatting about old times while Scott went to the barn to catch up with Tank. When Kyle asked if Scott was around, Peter went to the barn to go get him. A few minutes later Peter and Scott came back into the living room. Kyle stood and then addressed the room.

"I'm sorry, but is there somewhere we can talk a little more privately." Scott agreed but Bobbie shook her head.

"Anything you have to say to me, you can say in front of my family." Kyle looked at Scott who shook his head in agreement. They all sat down but the tension was getting thick.

"I have to apologize again for not getting Lionel's message in time. A few months ago we wrote up his will and he left everything to Scott, since he didn't know about you at the time." Everyone just kind of shook their heads in agreement and let him continue. "As I was saying, I didn't get Lionel's messages about changing his will until I hit land again. By that time, he had already passed." Kyle stopped to let this all sink in.

Peter, who was also a lawyer, understood immediately what he was trying to say. Because Kyle was not able to write up a new will before Lionel died, Bobbie inherited nothing. Peter walked over to sit closer to Bobbie to help her and let her know that he was still there. It took a little while longer for the others to understand what he was trying to say. Lynn spoke up first.

"You mean even though he told multiple people what his wish was, Bobbie gets nothing since he passed away before he could sign anything?"

"Yes." Both Peter and Kyle said at the same time.

Bobbie inhaled quickly as she understood what was being discussed. She excused herself and ran to where they had just buried Lionel. She sat on her daddy's grave and cried. She cried for what seemed like hours, but was only a few minutes.

"Dad I am so scared. I don't know what to think or how to act. I miss you already. I hate mom for keeping us apart. I don't understand how she could keep me from you. I need you. What do I do? I love it here. Knowing how close I was to owning this beautiful ranch that was owned by my dad, and then losing it. I don't think I can stay to have that reminder all the time. I have some thinking to do. I was already planning on moving to the ranch since I would own half of it. With living on the ranch and the money you left us, I wouldn't need to work, so I was going to call tomorrow to let my bosses know I wasn't coming back. I would have missed Lynn and Peter, but we could always visit each other. I can't believe that they're leaving so early tomorrow morning. But Peter has a meeting that he's been putting off. Lynn needs to go back to work too. I feel bad that they stopped their lives just for me, but I am also thankful they were here."

Lynn had walked up to Bobbie as she was still crying.

"Bobbie, I don't want to scare you. I just wanted to check on you. I had to fight Scott off. He tried to come, but I pulled the sister card." Bobbie could barely manage to give a small smile. "So I heard some of what you said, but not all. Just so you know, I would give up my company if it means being there for you. You are my sister. Dad feels the same way. You're his second daughter. We both want to be there for you more, but you are one stubborn girl. Don't ever feel like you are a burden. Now let's talk about all the stuff I didn't hear." Bobbie gave Lynn a long tight hug letting go of all the emotions she has been trying to hold in.

"It is not fair. Mom knew he was a good man and she still kept me from him. I could have grown up here and not have had to work so hard. I'm so lost right now. I have no idea where to go from here. I came here to meet my dying dad and learned I will now own half of this beautiful land, only to have it taken from me. I don't think I can stay here." Lynn just sat quietly letting her get it all out. After taking some deep breaths, Bobbie admitted to Lynn. "I slept with Scott." Lynn got a smile on her face.

"Girl, I want all the details. How was it? Was he big? I bet he was. I can guarantee he was better than Bruce, but I need confirmation from you." Bobbie gave a small giggle.

"Calm down. You are such a gossip whore." They both laughed knowing Lynn loved to hear and share everything. "So of course he was way better than two-pump Bruce. Girl, I never understood what you were talking about, but I now understand when you say toe curling." Lynn screamed in excitement.

"Girl yes. Toe curling sex is the best sex." Bobbie got quiet again.

"I think I might have feelings for him. What if I am only a convenient fuck for him?" Lynn assured her that was not the case.

"If you would have seen the fight we just had, there would be no doubt that boy has those feelings too. I had to remind him that we flew from Colorado to be with you and he hogged you this whole week. I've barely talked to you all week." Bobbie realized then how little they'd spent together.

"I'm so sorry. I've been so busy getting everything ready." Lynn stopped her.

"No. We are not here so you can entertain us. We are here for you. Like now, you need to break down and I want to be the one to hold you. Besides I may have been able to hang around with my own cowboy. Let me tell you, these Texas guys sure know how to kiss. Too bad it was only the one, and it was to make his ex back off. But I'll kiss that man anytime he wants. Just thinking about it is making me hot. Lets change the subject before I do something stupid like go to his cabin." Bobbie laughed because that was something she could see Lynn doing.

"Well, since I'm no longer going to be able to afford not to work, I guess I need to go back to Colorado in the morning with you and Peter. I'm sure your dad will let me ride in his plane since he owns it." Lynn looked at Bobbie

"If that's really what you want, then of course you can fly back with us. But Bobbie, you should really think about this." Bobbie just shook her head unable to say anything else. "Let's get back before Scott sends an army to look for you." As they walked slowly back, Bobbie told Lynn not to say anything to anyone about her leaving.

Scott and Peter were still talking to Kyle about the different things they could maybe do, but each person had a reason it wouldn't work. No one noticed when they walked in the kitchen, so Bobbie went straight upstairs and started to pack her bags. It's not like she had a lot. Once that was done she went back downstairs to let them know that she was going to bed. Kyle let himself out and the others made their way to the bedrooms. Once again Scott grabbed Bobbie and led her into his room.

"We're going to get this all worked out, I promise." Scott said as they climbed into his bed. Bobbie just nodded.

"Scott, I need you tonight." She pressed her lips to his.

"Yes." He growled, taking over and deepening the kiss. He undressed her slowly and gently made love to her.

It was different this time, none of the usual urgency. Bobbie was determined to memorize every second. The way Scott's hands caressed her body, the heat of his mouth against hers, the feeling of him moving inside of her; it was all perfect. All she could think about was how she wanted this every night of her life. When she came, it was an extremely passionate and explosive moment; nothing had ever felt better. But it was also bittersweet. This would be the last time for them and she knew she'd never find anything like this again. This wasn't her home and Scott didn't belong to her; the best thing to do would be to go.

Bobbie didn't tell Scott she was leaving in the morning. Instead she waited for him to fall asleep and then she wrote him a note.

Dear Scott,

Thank you for looking me up when you found that letter. I'm still not sure why my mother never introduced me to my father, but I'm so lucky to have met him before he passed; even for the short time we had. He will always be a part of me no matter what. I also want to thank you for being you. You have been nothing but kind and generous to me since I showed up in that hospital room. I have felt at home on this ranch since the first time I stepped foot on the ground. Kind of like I belonged here. I don't hold Mr. Bradshaw responsible for how everything ended. It is what it is. I'll miss this ranch. If you do some of those ideas we talked about I know this ranch and city would grow even more. I'm sorry I have to leave you a note. I'm not sure I would be able to say all this to your face. I'm not sure about you, but I felt something for you. From the moment we met in the hospital, I just felt connected to you. Not sure how you felt. Since my bills are all paid off I have decided to only work one job and move to a safer neighborhood when I go back to Colorado. I hope you have a great life and keep in touch.

Love, Bobbie

Bobbie left the letter on her pillow and then made her way to the front door where Peter and Lynn were trying to stay quiet.

"Oh sorry baby girl, we were trying to keep it down so we did not wake you up" Peter whispered.

"You didn't wake me up, I set my alarm so I could go back with you. If that's okay, or I can go to the airport and go home on a commercial plane." Bobbie replied.

"No way are you flying home by yourself. Are you sure you want to go back? Scott and Kyle are still looking for ways to change his will." Peter stated. Bobbie just shook her head yes and walked to the black car that was waiting for them.

CHAPTER 14

It had been three weeks since Bobbie came back to Colorado. She quit the restaurant and only worked at the bowling alley. She was looking for a new apartment. It was nice to not have to worry about money so much. Lynn went back to work and so did Peter. It was almost as if Texas never happened. Peter called one day to tell her he was looking into getting her half of the ranch, but it would take time since he knew Colorado laws and some of Texas laws were different.

"Don't worry about it Peter. I appreciate all you have done and I'm so thankful that you took the time off to be there for me."

"Anything for you baby girl, you know that. Hey do you need anything; money, food, anything I can help you with?" Peter asked, figuring she would turn him down like usual. But to his surprise she said yes.

"You know what I could use? Remember when you used to take Lynn and I to that pizza joint to cheer her up after whatever drama happened to unfold that day? I could go for a cheer up pizza, if you're not too busy?" Before she could backpedal her way out of it, Peter jumped at the chance.

"You got it baby girl. Let me tell Lynn that dinner is on me tonight. I'll pick you up around six thirty."

They hung up the phone and Bobbie got back to work. Since she quit working at the restaurant she had picked up a lot more hours at the bowling alley. The manager was looking for an assistant, but since no one could put in the hours she hadn't hired anyone. Now she was looking to promote Bobbie. It was getting late so Bobbie clocked out and headed home to shower. She was washing her hair and didn't hear the phone ring. When she was finished dressing Peter was knocking on her door. As they were getting into his car her home phone rang, but she decided to let the answering machine get it. Lynn gave Bobbie a huge hug as soon as she got in the car. They were all talking about their day on the way to the pizza place. At the pizza parlor, they ate and laughed, having a great time. Peter and Bobbie started to reminisce about each reason that they came here to cheer up Lynn over the years.

"Hey, you two are making me sound spoiled." Peter and Bobbie stopped laughing and looked at each other. Then all three burst out into full blown belly laughs that had nearby tables looking their direction. Peter got serious for a moment.

"Hey do you girls remember what happened when pizza just did not cheer Lynn up?"

"ICE CREAM!" Both girls shouted. This got the rest of the pizza joint to stop talking and everyone looked their way. They got up and threw away their trash.

"Okay ladies are we walking or driving to the ice cream place?" asked Peter. Bobbie and Lynn each grabbed one of his elbows and led him walking down the street to the ice cream parlor. They continued to laugh and joke about old times. When they got to the ice cream parlor, Bobbie ordered the rocky road, Lynn ordered the buttered-pecan and then Peter ordered lime sherbet; all with three scoops.

"Gross." Both Lynn and Bobbie cried together.

"Okay change that to mint chocolate chip." Peter looked at both girls for approval before he paid the cashier. Each of them grabbed a couple of spoons and their bowls and they sat outside. They each ate a scoop of each flavor. They had done this as long as Bobbie could remember.

They sat and talked and laughed. Once they were finished with the ice cream, Peter called for the car. As they headed home Peter asked Bobbie what she had been doing lately.

"Well I quit the restaurant and I have been full time at the bowling alley. I'm looking for a better apartment but still within my budget. I can't believe that my father, whom I barely met, would just pay off all my debt. I feel so free without the bill collectors calling and notices coming in every month." Peter gave Bobbie a sideways hug.

"You know baby girl, I would have been more than happy to pay off all your debt also. You never allowed me to do anything for you. I think I'll take a page out of your father's book next time and just do it. Forget asking you, just do it."

"Please don't do that. I hate owing people."

"Owing is when you borrow, but accepting something is a gift." Peter just laughed.

A short time later, they pulled up to Bobbie's apartment and there was a man standing at the door. Peter got out, making sure it was safe, before he allowed Bobbie to get out. When he noticed that it was Scott standing there, he leaned back in the car.

"Bobbie I think it's safe for you to go ahead, however, if you want we can come in with you." Bobbie looked over his shoulder to see Scott standing there.

"I'm sure that I'll be fine, but why don't you come on up anyway to say hi." Peter, Lynn, and Bobbie walked over to Scott. "Hey, come on up." Bobbie told Scott. The four of them made their way up to Bobbie's apartment. "I know it's not much, but it was all we could afford at the time." Bobbie tried to explain to Scott as she unlocked the door. They entered and sat, all quietly waiting for someone to start. Scott cleared his throat.

"I um… tried to call you earlier but you never answered. I took a cab here and tried your door. When no one answered, I decided to wait for you. If you didn't come in an hour I was going to get a hotel room and try again tomorrow. I need to talk to you about moving back to Texas." Lynn and Bobbie both gasped at the same time. Peter just sat there and waited to hear everything.

"I'm sorry Scott, but I told you how I felt. I can't be that close to the ranch and not be a part of it. Working it is not the same." Scott stopped her.

"I know exactly how you feel. I won't lie, when I found you and you actually showed up, I knew he wasn't going to leave the ranch to me after all. I thought about leaving. I don't think I could have done it though. I would never be happy unless I was on that land." Peter gave Scott a questioning look. Lynn was just holding Bobbie's hand. Scott stood up and pulled some papers from his back pocket and handed them over to Peter. "I assume you'll be her legal representative? You might want to see these." Peter looked over all the paperwork as Scott looked at Bobbie.

"These give you half of everything." He told her. Peter pulled out a pen and handed the papers over to Bobbie.

"Baby girl, I do believe these papers are in your best interest to sign." Bobbie opened the papers with Lynn reading over her shoulder; she began to softly cry.

"You mean? How did? Why?" Bobbie cleared her throat and Lynn squeezed her hand. "Scott, the ranch and everything was already in your name. Why would you give me half of every-thing? I thought Kyle said there was nothing he could do?" Bobbie stopped talking and just looked at Scott like he was crazy. Scott scooted closer to her.

"Bobbie, you were always supposed to have half. That's the way Old Man wanted it. When Kyle said there was nothing he could do, he meant nothing *he* could do. He explained that once it was all in my name I could do with it what I wanted. I wanted to do what was right. Please Bobbie, tell me you will come home with me. You said you were starting to have feelings for me. Guess what? I have those same feelings toward you. I want to start a life with you. Please Bobbie, I love you." Bobbie gasped

"What?" Scott just continued on as if she did not say anything.

"I can't live without you. The house is too quiet and my bed is too big." At this Peter cleared his throat.

"That might be a little more than we need to hear. Lynn, maybe we should go and let these two talk this out. Bobbie, I read those papers and I think you should sign them. If you do decide to go back to Texas please know that we will always be here for you, no matter what." Peter and Lynn left and Scott and Bobbie continued their discussion.

"Come back to Texas with me Bobbie."

"I don't know. My life is here. I have been doing really well these last three weeks. I'm down to one job and I think I have a real shot at running the bowling alley." She told him.

"Or you could run a ranch." Scott reminded her.

"Lynn and Peter are here." She quickly came up with another excuse.

"Peter and Lynn are more than welcome to come and visit for as long as they wish. Are those your only reasons?" She shrugged one shoulder. "Can you think of any reasons that you should go?"

"Well, I felt like I belonged in Texas the moment I stepped foot on that ranch. I fell in love with the ranch hands and some of the community. My father wanted me there."

"Anything else?" He wondered.

"Well, you're there." Their eyes locked. "Tell you what, why don't we go to bed? In the morning we can decide and discuss it with Peter." Scott got a big smile on his face.

"That is a great idea." Scott and Bobbie walked into her bedroom and fell on her bed. "I missed you Bobbie." Scott said as he stroked her face. He gently pulled her into a quick kiss.

"I missed you too." Bobbie murmured just before he claimed her lips. It wasn't the usual slow exploration, this was all heat, longing, and need. His mouth was demanding and possessive against hers.

Pulling her head back just far enough to look into her eyes, "Why did you leave me?" He asked the question burning in his mind. "I told you we would figure this out."

"I just thought it was time for me to get back to my reality, where I belong." Bobbie shrugged looking down. Scott gently lifted her chin and forced her to look at him again.

"You want to know what your reality actually is Bobbie?." He ran his thumb over her bottom lip. "It's that you belong in Texas, on the ranch, with me."

"With you?" She echoed.

"Damn right with me." He kissed her lightly then whispered in her ear. "How could you not know that I was falling for you?"

"Because I was scared." Bobbie admitted. "I've never felt anything like I felt for you. Ever. And it scared me to death. I just kept thinking that there was no way that you could feel the same way. How could you? I'm completely lost and a little bit of a mess right now. But you, you're perfect. You're gorgeous, smart, and fun. You completely have your life under control. You know exactly what you want and you work hard to get it."

"You're right about that baby. And what I want is you." He pressed his lips back to hers, tongue seaking entrance to her mouth. When she parted her lips, he wasted no time deepening the kiss. When they finally broke apart, Scott whispered. "Come home with me Bobbie. I'm completely miserable without you."

"Really?" Bobbie's eyes were wary. "Why didn't you come after me sooner?"

"God I wanted to. It was my first thought when I woke up to that damn letter." Bobbie blushed guiltily, that was exactly how her mother had left her father. "I threw some stuff in a bag and jumped in my truck to follow you. I got to the airport but I couldn't get a flight for two days. I didn't know what to do. I thought about driving all the way to Colorado, but when I got back in the truck, all my doubts came rushing over me. I started thinking about how I'm not good enough for you and…" Bobbie tried to interrupt.

"That's not…" But Scott raised his hand to hush her.

"And then I thought that maybe you wouldn't want me coming after you. That maybe this was all just some kind of fling for you, something to get you through your grief. That if you wanted me at all, you would have stayed. I mean, you just left. You didn't even say goodbye or give me the chance to beg you not to go." There was hurt and insecurity in his eyes.

"I'm so sorry Scott. I never meant to hurt you. Or make you think that I don't want you."

"Yeah, well." Scott sighed. "It still happened." Bobbie started to speak, but he pressed a finger to her lips. "Anyway, I went home and kind of lost myself in a bottle for a few days."

"Oh Scott." She knew from their late night conversations that he didn't really drink because of his parent's problems with alcohol.

"Yeah, it was pretty bad. But Tank was there to kick my ass back into shape. And Randy was there to help me man up, do what I needed to do to try to get you back." He caressed the side of her face. "It was the legal stuff that took the longest. Kyle did all he could to speed up the process, but I had to wait until the ranch was mine before I could sign half over to you."

"I still can't believe you did that." Bobbie shook her head.

"I love you Bobbie. I would do anything for you. I want to give you everything you deserve. Be everything you need."

"You are." Bobbie assured him, pressing their mouths together in a deep passionate kiss which soon turned up the heat between them.

"God I missed this." Scott murmured against her lips. "Missed you."

Bobbie said nothing; simply kissed him again and pulled him on top of her. He was already hard against her, which caused her to moan. Heat spread through her body and she yanked at his tee shirt, needing to feel his muscled chest under her hands. But that wasn't enough, would never be enough. She needed more, she needed all of him. He told her that he loved her and asked her to come back with him. He'd laid himself bare for her, but she couldn't think of the words to return the sentiment. So she tried to show him with her lips and roaming hands that this meant every-thing to her.

They undressed slowly, pausing frequently to kiss and wor-ship each bit of skin that they exposed. Naked, their hungry mouths returned to one another's until they're breathing out of control. Breaking the kiss, their lust blown eyes locked; stark need written on both their faces.

"Want you Scott." Bobbie panted. "So badly."

"Me too baby." Scott's hand tangled in her hair and held her in place for another blistering kiss. "Condom?" He asked, voice wrecked.

"I don't have any." Bobbie shook her head.

"Damn." Scott groaned. "I didn't bring any."

"I don't want to stop." She all but whined, kissing him again until they were both trembling with desire.

"What if you get pregnant?" He whispered the question in her ear so that she couldn't see the want in his eyes. He could see her flat stomach swollen with his child and the thought caused his heart to clench. Damn but he wanted that; a family and a future with the woman of his dreams. But he still had no idea what Bobbie wanted. He kissed the spot just below her ear that made her shiver and she moaned.

"Scott." Just that one word, his name spoken in such a desperate way, caused his control to snap and he slid inside of her. For Bobbie, it felt like coming home, like she was right where she was supposed to be and everything seemed to click into place for her. Scott was generous, loyal, and honorable; all the things she'd always wanted in a partner. And she was in love with him. And she knew she could trust him, knew that she could give him her heart and he would take care of it.

"Bobbie." He kissed her, over and over as their bodies fell into a hard, fast rhythm.

"God Scott." He angled his hips just right and had her chanting his name. "Scott. Scott. Scott."

"Fuck." He growled. He wasn't going to last much longer; he'd been too long without her touch. And the way Bobbie was going crazy wasn't helping. All the moaning and writhing, her soft small hands alternating between clutching at him and teasing him, the feeling of her tight wet heat around his sensitive shaft, had him on the edge far quicker than he would have liked.

"Scott." Her breathing was ragged. "I love you." She breathed out, then all but screamed as the best orgasm of her life ripped through her body. Her head fell back onto the bed, eyes fluttering shut, as she rode out wave after wave of pleasure.

"I love you too." His thrusts lost all finesse as he sped up. He'd been so close already and her body pulsing and clenching around him pushed him over.

"Scott." Bobbie gasped, feeling the rush of heat deep inside of her. Oh god, what if she did get pregnant? Before she even had a chance to freak out, a calmness washed over her. Scott would take care of her, she knew that. And if they did have a baby, it would be born into a loving home. That thought made her smile.

Scott flopped down onto the bed next to her and pulled her into his arms. For a while they just lay there. Bobbie loved the feeling of his heart beating under her hands as he tried to calm himself. Finally he tilted her head up so that he was looking into her eyes.

"Did you mean it?" He asked, uncertainty coloring his voice. "Or was that just sex talk?"

"I meant it." She smiled.

"I need to hear you say it again."

"I love you Scott."

"Thank god." He whispered, pulling her into a deep kiss. "I love you too. So much. And I need you to come back to Texas with me baby. I can't lose you again." Bobbie started to speak, but Scott cut her off with a kiss. "But I know this is a big decision. A man you barely know is asking you to give up your entire life for him."

"But it's the man that I'm completely in love with that's asking. It's just a lot to process." He could see the confusion in her eyes. Part of him wanted to push her, use her admission to press her into saying she'd come home. He forced himself to say the right words, the words that she needed to hear.

"I know. Maybe we should get some sleep and talk about this more in the morning. And I'll wait for as long as it takes you to decide."

"You will? What if I need some time to decide?"

"Then I'll wait. I'd love it if you said that you'd come home with me tomorrow, but I understand if you need time. I love you Bobbie, you're it for me. I would wait for you forever. I'm not saying that patience is going to be easy, but I want you to take all the time you need. I want you to be sure." He kissed her again then pulled the covers up over them. "We should sleep now baby."

CHAPTER 15

The next morning Bobbie woke up to the smell of bacon, eggs, and coffee. She went into the kitchen and Scott explained that he was making her breakfast in bed.

"I didn't know you knew how to cook. I thought Denise did all the cooking?"

"She does, but Old Man thought it was one of those life lessons I should learn. He always said, just because you don't have to cook doesn't mean you shouldn't know how to cook. Just don't expect anything baked. I'm not good at baking." Both Scott and Bobbie laughed.

They ate and talked more about her moving to the ranch.

"You know I had an idea to bring kids from the city to the ranch to experience horses." At first he was not sure, but she explained that living in the city all her life she never had a chance to touch a horse, much less ride one. He explained that the same thing happened to him. His parents were living in the city and before coming to the ranch he never had any experience with a horse. They also agreed that the poor should be able to experience horses and not just the rich who could afford riding lessons.

"I guess I need to make a decision about moving back to Texas. Do you mind if we stop and talk to Peter? I trust him more than myself with my big decisions."

"Not at all. I want you to be completely sure about this move. This is a huge decision and it shouldn't be made lightly. Just know that even if you decide to stay here in Colorado, you will still own half of everything. But while you're trying to make your decision, I want you to remember everything I told you last night. I love you Bobbie and I want nothing more than for you to come home with me."

They made their way to Scott's rental car and drove to Peter's office. As they walked in his secretary showed them right to Peter's door. Unless he was in a meeting, if Lynn or Bobbie ever stopped by she was to escort them straight to his office, no questions asked. When the door opened Peter looked up from his desk and stood up to greet Scott and Bobbie.

"What's going on baby girl?" Bobbie walked over to Peter and gave him a hug and a kiss on the cheek.

"Hey Peter, I just wanted to go over those papers with you one more time before I sign them. Then I wanted to hear your honest opinion on my moving to Texas or staying here in Colorado."

"Okay then, let's have a seat here on my couch." Bobbie sat next to Peter and Scott pulled up a chair.

They talked over each page and seemed to agree with everything. It was a basic contract detailing how Bobbie would own fifty percent of everything and Scott would own the other fifty percent. He'd kept in Lionel's clause that if either wanted to sell, they had to give the other first chance to buy out and it had to be at least fair market value. It also stated that in the event something should happen to one, the other half of the ranch would go to the other person. Lastly it stated that as long as the ranch could afford to, they had to keep on as many employees as possible. When they got to the last page Bobbie signed and Peter had his secretary fax it over to Kyle Bradshaw's office so he could get it documented at the courthouse and make it legal.

"Okay baby girl, my honest opinion is that if you do go back to Texas, you won't be there alone for long. I can see Lynn following you and with both my girls in Texas, what would I do here?

However, if you stay here, you can manage the bowling alley or you can buy your own bowling alley. You're now a rich woman. You might be able to buy me out now. Money is no longer an issue. The real issue is where your heart is."

"You have no idea how at home I felt there." Bobbie looked at Peter. "I really tried to make a life here, but I just feel so lost." Peter gave her a hug.

"Go home and pack." So that's what she did.

Scott and Bobbie were in the middle of discussing what to take and what to trash or donate when a knock came at the door. Bobbie answered the door just as Lynn was pushing it open. Lynn and Peter were there to help in any way they could.

"I hear you could afford to have people do this for you now." Lynn joked with Bobbie.

The four of them packed most of the apartment when Scott reached high into the closet and pulled a box down that was stuck way in the back.

"What is that?" asked Bobbie. Scott shrugged his shoulders as he opened the box. He looked inside and noticed a bunch of pictures of Lionel and Allison.

"Um… Bobbie maybe you should check this out." Scott handed the box to her and watched as she opened it.

"What is in it?" Lynn asked.

"Pictures of my parent's together." Bobbie answered with tears leaking from her eyes. There was also a note addressed to her. She set the letter aside and continued to go through the pictures. As she looked at each picture, she handed them to Scott, who handed them to Lynn, who handed them to Peter. There was one picture of Lionel and Allison on their wedding day.

"Hey Old Man still has this one in his room." Scott said out loud.

They continued to go through the pictures until the only thing in the box was her bridal ring set and a letter. Everyone pretended to be studying the pictures they were holding so Bobbie could have a few seconds to gather her strength.

"Lynn, do you think you can come sit with me as I open this letter? I know I'm being a big baby, but I'm kind of scared of what it might say." Lynn walked and sat next to Bobbie on the side of the bed.

"No problem sister, I'm here for you, however and whenever you need me." Very slowly Bobbie reached into the box and pulled out the wedding ring set and tried them on.

"Oh, look they fit. Maybe one day when I get married, I can wear this set. Peter can you hold these until then?" Peter reached for the rings and put them in his pocket.

"I'll be honored to hold onto these until they are handed to the man who deserves them." Peter gave Scott a pointed look.

Bobbie was too interested in the letter to take notice of the look. Taking a deep breath, she picked up the letter. She just stared at it for a few seconds and then slowly opened it.

Dear Bobbie Jean,

I love you more than you could ever know. If you are reading this I'm no longer living, but I can tell you that I still love you. This letter is so hard to write. Over the past I have fought with myself on why I refused to tell you about your father. The real honest truth is I didn't want to lose you. I loved your father very much and he loved me more than anything. I regret not staying and working things out, but I just couldn't. I lost my dad as a baby. My step dad tried to force himself on me when I was a teenager and was blessed enough to be able to live with my Aunt Linda. She lived in the country and I was born and raised a city girl. I worked at Aunt Linda's Diner and that is where I met your daddy. He was so handsome and sweet. He didn't flirt with any of the other waitresses, like so many of the other men did. He asked me out and I told him no at first. Don't ask me why, I guess I was playing hard to get. He never gave up and I finally gave in. We went to the fair grounds for our first date where he won me that striped teddy bear I love so much. He was my first love, my only love besides you. We married soon after and not a day went by that I regretted that. We got into married life fairly easy enough but something was missing. I wanted a family and he wanted me to have whatever made me happy. After a few years of trying, I was getting lonely so I asked your daddy if I could be a foster mom. That way I had a child to look after to help with the loneliness. Of course he agreed without much thought. That is the kind of man your father was. Whatever I wanted he gave me. It was probably close to a year when no one from the foster system called. I had called them and was told with us living so far away from town that we were one of the last options. So I sat there and cried that night. I was homesick for the city. I knew if I told your dad how I felt that he would have sold the ranch and moved into the city to make me happy. I didn't want him to have to give up his ranch because he would only be in the same position I was in. He would be homesick and I couldn't do that to him. I left your father and shortly after I found out I was pregnant with you. I was scared and alone and I made some bad choices. Trust me Bobbie Jean, if I could go back in time I would never have left your father. You must think I'm a crazy woman for giving up that life to live the life I shared with you. I still heard about your father from Aunt Linda. He never remarried nor had any other children of his own, but he took in a young boy. I wrote to him one time and told him about you. I swear I never heard from him after that. I sometimes wonder why he never came to look for us. I stayed in that house in that city for three years after I sent that letter. After that I thought I could fool myself into thinking that if we kept moving then I could blame the moves on him not finding us. However, I never found out why he never came. By now you were going to be a teenager and you wanted to settle down. I told you that I would think about it, but once I saw you with your little friend, Lynn Daniels, I knew I couldn't take you away from someone else again. I know that if I made sure your father got my letter that he would be here with you. However, I know that I couldn't go back to the ranch or he would want you to go live with him. I was selfish in keeping you away. I know this makes me a horrible mother and I only hope that one day you could forgive me. In this box are all the pictures I have of your father. I told you he was handsome. You look so much like him. I'll tell you his name now and if you still want to know him that is up to you. His name is Lionel James.

Love Mom

P.S. If you do happen to meet him one day. Can you tell him that I never stopped loving him.

Lynn and Bobbie had tears in their eyes and could hardly talk, so they just passed the note to Scott and Peter walked over to read it with him. Once the guys were done reading the letter, the girls had gotten their emotions under control.

"Okay, let's put this back in the box and finish packing. I need to get to the ranch so I can give my dad a message from my mom."

Epilogue

"Momma, are you sure my granddaddy is under all this grass?" James Scott Wilson asked.

"Yes." Bobbie answered, smiling at her two year old son. It had been about three years since Lionel James passed away and today they were going to celebrate his life. James took off running when he saw his Grandpa Peter. Scott walked up and hugged Bobbie.

"Wow what a difference three years can make." Scott whispered in Bobbie's ear.

Bobbie looked around and couldn't agree more. They now had a special spot where they bussed in city kids to learn their way around a ranch. They still had their original ranch hands, minus a couple who had left over the years. Plus they had to hire about fifteen more. They had built on to the house. Denise and Tank were married and now had twin daughters a year older than James. Old Man Henderson passed away and Peter bought his place. Lynn still had her company based out of Colorado, but she was making plans to move to Texas to live with her dad.

"I love you Scott, more and more each day." Bobbie turned to give Scott a hug. James came running to get his daddy.

"Daddy, Daddy, Grandma Wilson is here. She even brought me a present, but she said I have to wait for you to open it. Hurry

Dad, I want that present." Scott and Bobbie walked back towards the house. Once they walked into the kitchen Scott saw his mother, Betty.

"Hey mom. How are you doing?" Scott asked as he gave her a huge hug.

Shortly after Bobbie moved back to Texas, Scott met his mom for coffee. She explained that one day she woke up and just couldn't even look at herself in the mirror anymore. That day she packed a couple of outfits and left. She got a ride to the bank, took out half of whatever was in there and got a ride to the next town over. She got a job as a waitress and a small apartment then filed for divorce. Once that was all taken care of, she started going to AA meetings. It was there that she met a counselor who thought she needed to talk about more than her drinking and asked to discuss it over dinner. She agreed and had been seeing him since, both professionally and privately. They had taken their relation-ship slowly, but she was happy. Scott then met his mother once a month to talk, and then it was twice a month, and now they talked as often as possible and saw each other when they could.

"I'm doing great Scott, just wanted to show my daughter in law a little something, something." Betty said as she held her hand up to show Bobbie her engagement ring.

"Oh my Gosh that's so exciting. When's the wedding?" As soon as she finished her question there came a voice through the door.

"Who's getting married?" Bobbie turned toward the door and ran to give Lynn a huge hug.

"I can't believe you made it. I thought you said you were swamped at work." Lynn smiled.

"Again, I'm here for you whenever and however you need me. You're my sister. I'll always be here for you. Besides who else is going to be your maid of honor?" Both girls jumped and screamed in excitement. Peter tried to walk in the door but stopped when he saw the girls screaming.

"Come on girls, grow up a little, huh. Bobbie Jean, you are getting married tomorrow and you have a little boy; you should be ashamed of yourself carrying on like a child." Both girls stopped to look at him like he was crazy, then they looked at each other and both ran for Peter at the same time. Everyone was laughing and having a good time.

"So let's see what needs to be done before tomorrow." Lynn told Bobbie.

"Okay, Randy is in the barn trying to string the lights and then he's going to build the stage. Do you think you can go to the barn to help him?" Bobbie knew it would be a while before she saw Lynn again. Every time Lynn came to town she saw how Randy and her looked at each other; the same way she and Scott looked at each other.

Everyone was accounted for, since they had chosen to have a small ceremony. Peter was going to walk Bobbie down the aisle. Lynn was the maid of honor and Randy would be the best man. Denise and Tank were also going to stand up for them. James was going to be the ring bearer and Jessa and Jenna, Tank and Denise's twins, were both going to be flower girls.

That night Scott was at Tank's house with all the kids and Denise and Lynn were at Bobbie's house. They had a girl's night. When Lynn popped open a bottle of wine, Bobbie declined.

"Oh come on girl, you are kid free for the whole night. Live free for once." Lynn told Bobbie. Bobbie kept declining the drink and then when they passed around a plate of tuna on crackers, Bobbie ran for the bathroom. Suddenly both Lynn and Denise knew why she declined. Once Bobbie came back she tried to play it off as if she just had to pee really bad, but Lynn was not buying it.

"Okay so am I the last to know? Is that it? Because I haven't moved to Texas yet, you are going to hold back on telling me I'm going to be an aunt again. I see how it is." Bobbie's eyes met Lynn's with that deer in the headlights look.

"I never said anything to you because I think I should tell Scott first, but since you're a hound dog for gossip. I'll admit that I am pregnant. But please don't tell anyone else until after my honeymoon when I tell my husband." At first Lynn and Denise just looked at Bobbie. Then they both jumped up to hug her and they all three were screaming in excitement. They spent the rest of the night thinking of ways to surprise Scott with the news.

The next day as everyone was getting ready; Lynn excused herself from the bride's room. She and Randy had made a plan to secretly meet in the barn. Since she had been in Texas this weekend, they have found different ways to be together without anyone noticing. Or so they thought. Scott knew exactly why Randy was sneaking around and Bobbie knew where Lynn was sneaking off to. Randy and Lynn had no idea that Scott and Bobbie set up little things for them to get alone time. Like that time that Scott had Randy walk to see if Lynn was going to need a ride to the store right after Bobbie asked Lynn to go to the store to get her something she forgot. Bobbie didn't forget anything, but it gave Lynn and Randy time alone. An hour before the wedding Lynn was back from the barn and was getting her hair and makeup fixed. Lynn's phone rang and Bobbie answered it.

"Hello this is Lynn's phone, Bobbie speaking."

"Hey Beautiful. I'm so sorry I'm unable to make your wedding. I did send you something and you should be getting it next week."

"Oh thanks Bryan, that's so sweet. I'm sure I'm going to like it. So when are you coming to visit Texas?"

"I'm kind of busy with college and work right now. But I promise I'll make a trip. I'll probably bring a couple of friends with me."

"That would be awesome. Peter lives two houses from me and I'm still trying to get Lynn to move here." Bobbie laughed and then handed the phone to Lynn so she could talk to her cousin.

Since Bobbie and Lynn were so close, Bobbie met Bryan when he came to visit for the summers. He used to spend his spring break with them every year, but this year he was going to move away for college. Lynn chatted with Bryan for a few minutes and then she told Bobbie that Bryan wanted to come for a visit during spring break. They talked a little until Peter knocked on the door.

"Are you ready baby girl?" James then ran into the room.

"Aunt Lynn I need the rings to put on my pillow. I'm the ring bearer." Lynn laughed at how James was standing all tall and acting like his having the rings was a major deal.

"Of course you are, little man. Here is the pillow with the rings, now remember you can't pull the strings until mommy or daddy asks you to, right?" Lynn waited until James agreed before pulling her hand from the pillow.

Suddenly music started to play and Lynn let her nephew know it was time.

James and the twins walked down the aisle followed by Denise and Tank. As Lynn and Randy walked down he asked her if she ever thought about her own wedding. She gave him a smile and whispered "yes" they each walked to their side of the stage. Peter held Bobbie back so he could talk to her.

"Baby girl." he started to say but choked up. Clearing his throat, he started again. "Baby girl, I have known and loved you most of your life. I know that if Lionel were here now he would say how proud he was of you. But since he's not here, I have that honor and let me tell you something. I have watched you grow from that scared little shy girl into a strong and confident woman. You have been through so much and you did it all on your own. You no longer have to do anything on your own. That man loves you and cares for you and it would make his day to be able to help you carry your burdens. I'll also be right by your side to help you both along. I love you baby girl and I'll always love you." With tears in her eyes Bobbie hugged Peter.

"I love you too Dad. Now let's go get me married." Peter loved that Bobbie had started to call him dad. They both laughed as they started to walk down the aisle. Peter had to pull her back a time or two when she was trying to hurry.

After the wedding and reception Lynn pulled Bobbie aside and asked if she was ready and if she knew how she was going to tell Scott. Bobbie laughed and said that she was going to play it by ear. Then Bobbie made sure that Lynn was going to stay in town for the week to watch over James. They made a plan to have a girls day when she got back to talk about the details and stuff before Lynn had to leave back to Colorado.

Scott and Bobbie decided to get a honeymoon suite in San Antonio, Texas. They didn't want to go too far from the ranch since James had never been away from them before. Once they were in the room, Scott ordered room service. He was helping Bobbie out of her wedding gown; he assumed there were over a hundred little buttons on that dress. By the time he finally finished the last button, there was a knock on the door. Scott opened the door so room service could bring in their dinner. They served food at the wedding, but it was so busy. They were trying to dance and say thanks to their family, and do this and that. It seemed by the time they got to sit down, the dinner portion was over. They both sat at the table and were talking about what a nice wedding it was. They were surprised by a couple of people actually showing up, but they were happy to see them.

"Did you see Steve tonight? He kept hanging around Tank all night." Bobbie asked. The two were so rushed that they probably missed half the people that were there.

Once they were almost done, Scott got up and started a warm bath for Bobbie. He again helped her undress and held her hand while she got into the tub. Once she was situated he undressed, grabbed the bottle of wine and two glasses. He slid into the tub behind her and set the bottle and glasses down. He grabbed a sponge and started to slowly wash her back. The whole time he would place kisses all over her back. When he was done, he grabbed the glasses and poured them each some wine. When Bobbie declined he explained that they were kid free and that she should drink so they could celebrate. That was when she told him.

"We're not exactly kid free." Scott looked at her funny. Then he looked around the bathroom then back at her. She could tell the second he understood her meaning. He looked at her with a smile then towards her stomach and then back at her. With each second his mouth was getting a bigger smile.

"You mean. Are you? Are we having another baby?" The hope in his voice was too much and with Bobbie's eyes tearing up she shook her head yes. "Oh my god baby. I'm so excited. I was actually going to ask you tonight if you wanted to start trying to have another baby. I'm so happy. I hope this one's a girl." Scott couldn't stop talking, his mouth was just running away. He was so happy. "When we get home I'll add on to the house so each child can have their own room. Maybe I should add two more rooms while I'm at it." Bobbie laughed.

"We'll discuss that later. Right now, we have a honeymoon to start."